Box Car Children Series tub

THE BOXCAR CHILDREN HALLOWEEN SPECIAL

THE MYSTERY OF THE SINGING GHOST

THE MYSTERY OF THE MUMMY'S CURSE

THE MYSTERY AT SKELETON POINT

created by
GERTRUDE CHANDLER WARNER

ALBERT WHITMAN & Company
Morton Grove, Illinois

The Boxcar Children Halloween Special
created by Gertrude Chandler Warner.

ISBN 978-0-8075-0884-8

For more information about Albert Whitman & Company,
visit our web site at www.albertwhitman.com.

Contents

THE MYSTERY OF THE SINGING GHOST

created by

GERTRUDE CHANDLER WARNER

Illustrated by Charles Tang

Albert Whitman & Company
Morton Grove, Illinois

The Mystery of the Singing Ghost
created by Gertrude Chandler Warner;
illustrated by Charles Tang.

ISBN 978-0-8075-5398-5

Contents

CHAPTER 1

The Old House

The Alden children and their cousins Joe and Alice Alden stood in front of an old house on the edge of Greenfield. They looked up and down at the three-story, gray-shingled home. It needed painting. The porch steps were broken and the windows on each of the three floors were a different shape.

Six-year-old Benny shook his head. "This sure is a funny-looking house," he said.

Joe laughed. "I guess it is. But this house

was built in 1900 and in those days houses didn't look like they do now."

Joe's wife, Alice, walked up the four steps that led to the wide porch. "The real estate agent gave me the key," she said. "Let's go in."

The children followed Alice inside. They all walked through the dusty living room and dining room. Ten-year-old Violet ran her fingers over an old table that was in the living room. "This place could use a good dusting," she said.

Henry, who was fourteen, said, "Well, I heard the agent tell Joe and Alice that no one has lived in the house for years."

They all walked into a small room with walls covered with empty bookshelves. A huge desk that took up half the room was against one wall. A dead plant was on the floor.

Jessie said seriously, "In all my twelve years I've never seen a place as strange as this one."

Alice moved toward the door. "We haven't

even been upstairs yet. Come on, let's look."

As they walked up the stairs, every step creaked. "Are you *really* going to buy this house?" Benny asked.

They went through all four bedrooms. Two of them still held some furniture. Alice peered out of a window onto an overgrown garden. "You know, Joe," she said, "with some work this might be just right for us."

"I don't think this house is right for anyone," Benny said. "It's dirty and creaky and it smells funny, too."

Joe looked around again. "We'll have to think about this, Alice. I'm just not sure."

They all left the house, and the door squeaked loudly as Alice closed it. "I don't think *I'd* like to live here," Violet said. "It's creepy."

When Henry's foot went through the wood of one of the porch steps, they all laughed. "I said it needed some work," Alice said.

When the Alden family reached the front walk, they noticed an old, white-haired man cutting the hedges that separated his house from the one they'd just been in.

The old man sniffed and said, "Looking at the old Roth house?"

"What's a Roth house?" Benny asked.

The old man snorted. "Roth! Roth! That's the name of the man who built the house you just came out of."

"Oh!" Benny said.

"I'm Charles Farley," the white-haired man said. "I live here. Who are you?"

The Aldens introduced themselves one by one. "We're thinking of buying the Roth house," Alice said.

"Are you *really*?" Violet asked.

"Now, Alice," Joe said, nervously, "we have to talk about that."

"If I were you young people, I'd *never* buy that old place. *Never!* Take my word for it," Mr. Farley said, firmly.

"I wouldn't buy it either," Benny said.

Alice walked closer to Mr. Farley. "Why would you never buy it. Do you think it's overpriced?"

Mr. Farley snorted again. "Who cares about the price? I wouldn't buy it because it's *haunted*."

"*Haunted!*" the Alden children all said at the same time.

Alice Alden laughed. "That's silly. Haunted by what?"

Mr. Farley narrowed his eyes. "By a ghost, of course."

Henry didn't believe in ghosts, but he wanted to be polite. "Whose ghost is it?"

Benny was wide-eyed. "Yes. Whose ghost is it?"

Mr. Farley started trimming the hedge again. "It's the ghost of young Celia Roth. She lived in that house with her father until 1917. Her mother had died when Celia was a baby. Then Celia just disappeared. No one ever did find out what happened to her. Her father never spoke of her again."

"How old was she when she . . . disappeared?" Violet asked timidly.

"Seventeen," Mr. Farley said. "Just seventeen. And no one ever found her — "

Alice looked at Benny and Violet's faces and interrupted Mr. Farley. "We have to go now. Children, come along."

They all piled into Joe and Alice's station wagon and headed home. Alice silently drove the car for a while and then said, "Kids, you know there are no such things as ghosts, don't you?"

Joe agreed. "You all know that, of course."

"Of course we do," Jessie said.

"Of course," Henry said.

But Benny and Violet were silent.

Joe and Alice dropped the children at their home. Joe said, "We're going on to Pine Grove. We have some big decisions to make. But first we'll stop by and give the key to the Roth house back to Mrs. Thaler, the real estate agent."

That night at dinner, the children told Grandfather about their visit to the Roth house. Henry was helping Mrs. McGregor carry a platter of chicken and bowls of little potatoes and peas in from the kitchen.

He took his seat at the table and said, "Can you imagine anything sillier than thinking a house is haunted?"

Grandfather laughed. "Well, of course it's silly, but I hope you were polite to Mr. Farley."

Benny looked at his grandfather. "You mean it? There really are no ghosts *anywhere*?"

Mr. Alden reached over and patted Benny's hand. "I really mean it," he said. "I hope you're not frightened."

"Not me!" Benny said firmly.

"Not me," Violet agreed.

The children all felt safe with Grandfather. They could hardly believe they had once run away from him. After their parents had died, they had heard that their grandfather was a mean man who wouldn't be nice to them. They had lived in a boxcar, until Mr. Alden had found them and took them and their boxcar back to his estate. Now the children couldn't be happier, and they loved their grandfather dearly.

When Mrs. McGregor brought in a big chocolate cake for dessert, Benny said, "I feel sorry for the ghosts. They'll never get to eat one of Mrs. McGregor's cakes. I think I'll eat an extra piece for them."

Mrs. McGregor sliced the cake and put two pieces on Benny's plate. "There you are, Benny," she said.

Just as they were all eating the cake, the phone rang. "I'll get it," Mr. Alden said and he walked into his study. He was on the phone for about five minutes before he returned to the dining room.

"Well, that was Joe. They've decided to buy that old house and move to Greenfield. They've already spoken to Mrs. Thaler, the agent," Grandfather said.

"The haunted one?" Benny asked.

"Come on, Benny. You know it isn't haunted," Mr. Alden said. "Aren't you happy Alice and Joe will be living here?"

Benny thought for a minute. "Yes, I am, but I'll miss going to the amusement park that's near where they live now."

"Well," Mr. Alden said, "I'll certainly be glad to have them here."

"When will they move in?" Jessie asked.

"Soon," Grandfather said. "I'm going to ask my lawyer to move things along quickly. They'd like to be settled in a couple of weeks."

"That place certainly needs a lot of work," Mrs. McGregor said as she brought in a bowl of fruit.

Jessie said, "Maybe *we* can fix it up a little."

Violet jumped up from the table. "What a wonderful idea! We could dust and clean out the closets and drawers. I noticed there were still things in some of them."

"We can oil the doors and windows," Henry said.

"And weed the garden," Benny added.

"And touch up some of the paint," Jessie said.

"I think Joe and Alice will be very happy to have you do all that," Grandfather said. "I'll pay for whatever supplies you need, of course."

"We'll need the key to get into the house," Henry said.

Mr. Alden nodded. "I'll call Mrs. Thaler in the morning and tell her to give you children the key."

"Can we take Watch?" Benny asked, looking at the Alden's dog, who was dozing in a corner.

Everybody laughed. "I don't think Watch would be much help," Grandfather said. "You'd better leave him at home."

"We'll take Watch some other time, Benny," Henry added, seeing Benny's disappointment.

Benny sighed. "I guess he'd have more fun at home anyway."

CHAPTER 2

Work! Work! Work!

The next morning, the Aldens got up and fixed a breakfast of orange juice, cold cereal, toast with strawberry jam, and milk. When they had eaten and cleaned up the kitchen, they ran down to the box-car.

It was almost the same as when they had lived in it. The only new things were the plump cushions Mrs. McGregor had made for the children to sit on. Now they made themselves comfortable on the pillows.

Benny pulled an apple out of his pocket and bit into it.

"Benny," Henry asked, "don't you ever stop eating?"

Benny grinned. "Yes — when I sleep."

"Okay," Jessie said, "let's make a list of everything we need to take to the old house."

"Well," Violet said, thoughtfully, "we need soap and rags and a mop . . ."

"And oil and paint and a paintbrush," Henry added.

"And, work gloves, and a broom and paper to line the drawers," Jessie said.

"And food," Benny said. "For us!"

"Okay," Jessie said. "We'll bike into town, buy all the stuff at the hardware store, and then we'll go to the market and get food for lunch. And then we can go to the 'Roth house,' as Mr. Farley calls it."

Henry said, "That's fine! Let's get our bikes and go."

Five minutes later the Aldens were biking down a tree-lined country road to the town of Greenfield. Once they reached the small town, they stopped at Mrs. Thaler's for the keys to the house. She handed Jessie two keys on a ring. "The larger one is for the front door and the smaller one is for the back door," she told them.

Then they rode over to Harmon's Hardware store. Mr. Harmon greeted them when they walked in. "Hi, Aldens. Can I help you?"

"We need a lot of cleaning things to take to the Roth house, which our cousins Joe and Alice are buying. We're going to help fix it up for them," Benny said all in one breath.

Mr. Harmon laughed. "It will take an army to fix that place up . . . *and* get rid of the ghosts."

Benny and Violet exchanged looks. "Ghosts?" they said together.

"Come on, Mr. Harmon," Jessie said. "Don't joke like that."

Mr. Harmon glanced at Benny's pale face. "Sure! Sure! I'm just joking. Now what can I get you?"

Henry handed Mr. Harmon the list. Mr.

Harmon looked at it and said, "That's quite a load. Tell you what — I have a delivery out that way this afternoon. I'll drop all this stuff off at the Roth place for you . . . around one o'clock."

"Great!" Jessie said. "Thanks a lot."

"I'll just put it all on your grandfather's account," Mr. Harmon said.

Benny said, "Now we can go to the store for our lunch food."

The Aldens walked across the street to a small market. Henry took a shopping cart, and the four children walked through the aisles. Into the cart they put a loaf of whole wheat bread, a large package of cheese slices, juicy tomatoes, peaches, chocolate cookies, and two quarts of milk. Benny added potato chips, and Violet ran back for paper plates, cups, and plastic tableware.

After they had paid, they divided the food into two bags. Henry and Jessie each put one in their bike baskets. Then they all rode the couple of miles to the old house. As they got off their bikes, a middle-aged man and

woman were getting into a car parked in the street. The dark-haired woman stared at the Aldens and then walked over to them.

"We're the Aldens," Benny said quickly. "Our cousins Joe and Alice are buying this house." He carefully pointed to the Roth house.

"I'm Gloria Carter," the woman said. "I live next door to the Roth house."

The man came over to her and she introduced him. "This is my husband, David." She turned to Mr. Carter. "Dave, the Roth house has been sold to the children's cousins."

Mr. Carter slowly narrowed his eyes. "I don't need any neighbors," he said gruffly.

Gloria Carter put her hand on her husband's arm and said, "Now, David, it will be lovely to have new young neighbors. I'm delighted!" She smiled. "We're driving into Greenfield to shop now. Will you be here long?"

"We're going to start cleaning up," Jessie

said. "We'll be here a lot in the next few weeks."

"How nice," Mrs. Carter said. "Then I'll see you again." The Carters got into their car and drove off.

The Aldens took the bundles from the bike baskets and carried them up to the porch. Jessie unlocked the door and they went into the house. "She was a nice lady," Benny said.

"Yes," Violet said. "But *he* wasn't very friendly."

Henry laughed. "Oh, well, one friendly neighbor out of two is okay."

Inside the house Benny wrinkled his nose. "Like I said before, it smells."

Henry went to a window and pulled it up. "It's just a little stuffy. Let's open *all* the windows. Upstairs, too. That will help."

"I'll go upstairs with you, Violet," Jessie said. "Benny, you stay down here and help Henry."

Upstairs, the girls went into each room and

pulled the windows up. Jessie looked into the largest bedroom. "Look, Violet, there are still shades on these windows."

Violet shook her head. "Yes, and look at them. They're torn and dirty and faded. I wonder if these are the Roth's shades, or if anyone lived in this house after they moved out."

"We can ask someone," Jessie said. "Let's go downstairs and see where we should begin to clean."

The girls ran lightly down the stairs and joined their brothers, who were in the living room. "Where should we start?" Jessie asked.

"We can't start anywhere," Benny said. "We have no cleaning things."

Jessie laughed. "Oh, I forgot. You *are* smart, Benny."

Benny grinned. "Well, then, I'm smart enough to know since we can't clean, we can at least eat. Let's fix lunch."

Henry shrugged and began to laugh. "We might as well."

Suddenly there was a loud *bang* from upstairs. The Aldens all jumped. "What was *that*?" Benny asked, his eyes wide.

Violet moved closer to Jessie. "There's nobody here but us — is there?" she asked, her voice shaking.

"I don't know, but I'll go look," Jessie said bravely.

"I'll go with you," Henry said.

Henry and Jessie walked up the stairs slowly. "What do you suppose it was?" Henry whispered to Jessie. He took her hand and they went from room to room.

In the large bedroom a shade was lying on the floor. Jessie laughed. "*That's* what it was. That shade fell off the window. The wind must have done it."

Henry sighed with relief. "All this ghost talk. You know it gets to you."

"Are you all right?" Violet called from downstairs.

"We're fine," Henry called back. "A window shade fell on the floor. That's all."

"Good," Benny called out. "Let's eat."

The Aldens went into the kitchen and unpacked their food. "How come there are lights and water, if no one lives here?" Benny asked.

"Real estate agents often turn them on when they know they are going to be showing a house," Henry said. "Joe told me that."

The children made sandwiches of cheese and tomatoes and put them on the paper plates. Benny opened the chips and Violet passed around the fruit and cookies. After Henry poured the milk they sat on the floor in the kitchen and ate.

While they were eating there was a knock at the back door. "Harmon's," a voice called out. The delivery boy from the hardware store brought the boxes of cleaning things into the kitchen and put them on the floor. He glanced around the grimy room and said, "Boy, you sure have a lot of work to do." Then he left.

When the Aldens had finished eating, they put all the garbage into a paper bag. "I wonder if there's a garbage can around here," Jessie asked. She looked around the kitchen.

"What's behind that door?" Benny asked, pointing to a heavy wooden door next to the sink.

"I don't know — I didn't even notice it until now," Jessie said.

She pulled open the door and peered into the darkness. "No garbage can. But there's a staircase going up. Who wants to come with me?"

First there was silence, then Benny said, "I'll go," but his voice was just a little shaky.

Slowly Benny and Jessie walked up the flight of stairs. It was very dark, and Benny hung onto Jessie's hand tightly. They came to another door at the top of the stairs and Jessie opened it. They were in one of the bedrooms. She laughed. "It just leads up to the second floor."

"I thought so," Benny said.

Jessie lightly poked his arm. "I'll bet," she said.

The Aldens spent the afternoon working. Henry and Jessie scrubbed the kitchen. Violet dusted the living room and dining room, and Benny weeded the garden. After a couple of hours, they all admitted they were tired.

"Let's go home," Benny said.

"Yes, let's," Violet agreed.

They neatened up the cleaning supplies, carefully locked the back door, and went out the front door. They locked that, too.

Mr. Farley was in his yard mowing the lawn. He stopped when he saw the Aldens come out. "What have you been doing?" he asked.

"Cleaning and weeding," Benny answered. "So when our cousins move in, they won't have as much work to do."

"So, they *are* buying it," Mr. Farley said. "Foolish people. There is never enough room in one house for real live people *and* a ghost."

"We don't believe in ghosts," Jessie said.

"You will," the old man answered. "When

you hear Celia Roth singing, you'll believe in ghosts."

"Did you know her . . . Celia?" Violet asked timidly.

"I did," Mr. Farley replied. "I was just a boy when she lived here, but I remember her well. She was a beautiful, sweet girl. Maybe you'll see her someday, when you're in the house."

"Mr. Farley," Henry said, "I don't think we will."

Mr. Farley laughed. "We'll see," he said.

CHAPTER 3

The Singing

When the children reached home, they all went into the den and sat down. "You know," Jessie said, "I wonder whether Mr. Farley is deliberately trying to scare us. He talks about the ghost so much."

"Why would he want to scare us?" Violet asked.

"I have no idea," Jessie replied. "I just wonder. It seems strange to me."

"He isn't very nice, if he's trying to scare children," Benny said.

"I can't think of any reason why he'd do that," Henry said.

Jessie sighed. "I guess you're right. But that would mean he really believes there is a ghost."

"Maybe there is," Benny said.

"No," Henry said, "that's impossible."

But Benny was not convinced.

The Aldens went back to the house the next morning determined not to think about ghosts.

Henry started painting the porch railings. Violet and Benny got scissors and paper to line the drawers in the kitchen.

Jessie went upstairs to dust away the cobwebs in the bedrooms. Out one of the windows Jessie caught a glimpse of a man standing across the street, staring up at the Roth house. She stepped away from the window so he couldn't see her, and then peeked out again. The man was still staring at the house.

Jessie ran down the stairs and went outside

to Henry. "Look at that man across the street," she said to her brother.

Henry stopped painting and gazed at the man. Even though now the two children were looking at him, the man never moved.

"Let's go talk to him," Jessie said.

"What can we say?" Henry asked.

Jessie grabbed Henry's hand. "Come on," she said.

They walked across the street and Jessie said to the man, "Hi. Can we help you? You've been standing here quite a while."

The man frowned. "What's happening to this house?" he asked gruffly.

Henry smiled. "Do you know the Roth house well?"

"I'm Thomas Yeats," the man said. "I'm an artist. I've been working on a large picture of the Roth house. It's going to be my finest painting. I've been working on it for months, but it's not finished yet. So no one can change the look of the house."

Henry said, "Our cousins are moving in

here in a few weeks. They may change the house quite a bit."

Tom Yeats's voice was cold. "They *can't*. They *can't* make all my hard work useless. I'll put a stop to that." His eyes were blazing with fury. He turned and swiftly walked away.

"Wow!" Jessie said. "He was angry."

Jessie and Henry went into the house and told Violet and Benny what had happened. "That Mr. Yeats was really mad," Henry said.

"If the house starts to look different, can't the man just paint another picture?" Benny asked.

Violet shook her head. "Artists aren't like that," she answered Benny. "If Mr. Yeats has worked hard on that painting for a long time, he wants to finish it, not start something new."

"He sure was upset," Jessie said, remembering the sound of Mr. Yeats's voice.

Benny got bored with Mr. Yeats. "I have a good idea," he said. "Let's eat lunch out on the porch. I'll get the food Mrs. McGregor fixed for us this morning."

"Good idea!" Henry said. "I'll help you."

The Aldens all went into the kitchen, got the picnic basket Mrs. McGregor had packed, and took it out onto the porch. Henry spread newspapers on the floor, and the children sat down. From the picnic basket they took paper plates and cups, turkey sandwiches, purple plums, cookies, and a thermos of lemonade. They began to eat.

Suddenly they heard a voice coming from the house. Someone was singing! It was a girl, singing sweetly. The Aldens all stopped eating and listened. The voice was louder now, coming from upstairs. Henry jumped up and went to the door, and the others followed him.

"Who is it?" Benny asked, his voice quivering.

"Mr. Farley talked about Celia Roth singing," Violet said, moving closer to Jessie. Her eyes were wide.

"That *can't* be!" Jessie said.

"But *who* is singing?" Henry asked.

As suddenly as it had started, the singing stopped. Benny breathed a sigh of relief.

"I'm going to see what's going on," Henry said, heading toward the stairs.

"I'll go, too," Jessie said.

"I'm not staying here alone," Benny whispered.

"Me either," Violet added.

So all four Aldens went upstairs and tiptoed from room to room.

"There's nothing here," Jessie said.

"It must have been a radio," Henry said.

"But there isn't a radio in the house," Violet pointed out.

"And who turned it on if there was one?" Benny asked.

The Aldens were silent. There didn't seem to be any answers to the questions.

"Let's go home," Benny said firmly.

Jessie looked at Benny and Violet's worried faces and said, "We did a lot this morning. I think we should leave the house until tomorrow."

"Good!" Benny said.

The Aldens walked back downstairs and onto the porch. They finished eating their lunch, though no one was very hungry. Then they began to clean up the porch. They stopped their work when Mrs. Carter came up the walk.

"I just thought I'd see if I could help you," she said, smiling.

"We're just leaving," Jessie replied. "But thank you."

Mrs. Carter stared at the house with a funny expression on her face. "Mr. Carter and I would have bought this place and the property, but we couldn't afford it. I guess your cousins could." She looked longingly at the house.

"What does 'afford' mean?" Benny asked.

"It means having enough money to buy something," Mrs. Carter answered. "I envy your cousins."

Violet felt sorry for Mrs. Carter and a little unhappy. "I'm sorry, Mrs. Carter. But you'll like Joe and Alice."

Mrs. Carter smiled now. "Don't let me keep you. You seemed to be packing up. Knock on my door if I can help you anytime." She left.

The Aldens watched her walk away. Then Benny said, "Maybe she was the lady singing."

Jessie smiled. "Benny, she wasn't in the house. It couldn't have been Mrs. Carter."

Benny looked disappointed.

Henry said reassuringly, "It was probably a radio turned on somewhere. There are houses all around us. It just *sounded* as if it was coming from upstairs."

That night after everyone was in bed, Henry knocked on Jessie's door. She called out, "Come in."

Henry sat down on Jessie's bed. She looked up from her book.

"Jessie, things are sure funny at the Roth house," Henry said.

"*You* don't believe there's a ghost, do you?" she asked.

"Of course not," Henry said. "But something is going on. Mr. Farley keeps talking about ghosts. Mr. Carter doesn't want neighbors. Mr. Yeats is angry. Shades fall off windows. A girl is singing in the house, when there is no girl there."

Jessie thought for a minute. "None of what you said means anything is wrong. I'm sure all those things can be explained."

"But how?" Henry asked.

"I don't know," Jessie said. "But we'll figure it out. We always do."

Henry nodded. "I guess you're right." He smiled. " 'Night, Jessie."

After Henry left, Jessie sat very still and thought, Henry is right. Something *is* funny at the Roth house.

CHAPTER 4

The Argument

In the morning none of the Aldens felt like going right to the house.

Benny said, "Can't we go somewhere else first? We can clean in the afternoon."

"Benny's right," Violet said.

Jessie thought for a minute and then said, "I know. Let's go to the lake in the park. We can swim and then go to the house."

"Great!" Henry agreed.

"I think we should stop at the bakery first and buy some jelly doughnuts," Benny said.

Henry laughed. "Okay, Benny, we can do that."

The children biked into town and went to the bakery. Joan Bernstein, a tall, blonde woman who owned the shop, smiled when the Aldens came in. She looked away from the customer she was waiting on and said, "Hi, Aldens. I'll be with you in a minute."

She finished putting chocolate cookies into a bag and then said, "I think you children should meet Terry Evans." She gestured toward her customer, who was a short red-haired woman. "Ms. Evans is writing a book about the history of Greenfield."

"Is Greenfield that important?" Benny asked.

Ms. Bernstein nodded. "This town goes way back to colonial times."

Terry Evans smiled at the Aldens. "Have you all lived here very long?" she asked them.

"Since our grandfather found us and brought us here," Benny answered.

Ms. Evans laughed and started to leave the store.

"The Aldens' cousins have bought that old Roth house," Ms. Bernstein said. "The children are cleaning it up for them. Everyone in town is talking about how helpful the kids are."

Terry Evans turned to the Aldens. "Oh," she said. "I hear that's a very interesting house. Can you tell me about it?"

"We don't know that much," Jessie said hesitantly.

"You must know something," Ms. Evans insisted.

"Just that Mr. Farley says it's haunted," Benny said.

"But we know that's silly, of course," Henry added.

"Is it?" Ms. Evans asked. She looked at the children mysteriously. Then she said, "I have to go now, but I'd like to talk to you all again." Then she left.

Benny looked after her. "She liked us, I think. She wants to talk to us again."

"Yes, but why?" Henry asked. "We told her we don't know much about the house."

"She's just a very curious woman," Joan Bernstein said. "Now, what can I give you children?"

"Jelly doughnuts," Benny answered. "We're going to take them to the park."

Violet got four small containers of orange juice from the cooler, and Ms. Bernstein put the doughnuts, juice, and straws into a bag. The Aldens paid her and went out to their bikes. "Be careful at the lake," she called after them.

"We will," Violet called back.

When they reached the park, they sat on the grass under a tree. The shimmering lake was only a few yards from them.

Benny opened the paper bag and gave his brother and sisters a doughnut. Violet passed around the juice and straws. They sat contentedly and ate their snack, watching three teenagers playing in the lake.

They waited a little while after they had finished eating. Then they stripped down to the bathing suits they had on under their clothes. They ran to the lake and swam and splashed. Benny stayed near the shore. The Aldens kept their eyes on each other while they swam.

When they finally ran out of the water, they dried themselves and lay on the grass, talking softly. Suddenly, very close by, they heard loud voices. Under a nearby tree were Mr. Farley and Thomas Yeats. They hadn't seen the Aldens.

"I'll never do that. *Never!*" Mr. Farley cried out.

"I'm willing to pay you," Thomas Yeats said.

"No! It's not about money. I won't do it," Mr. Farley insisted.

"Forget it!" Mr. Yeats said, and he strode away. In a few seconds Mr. Farley left, too.

"Wow!" Violet said.

"What was that all about?" Jessie asked.

"What do you suppose Mr. Yeats wanted Mr. Farley to do?" Henry asked.

"Whatever it was, he was willing to pay for it," Violet said.

"Mr. Farley was certainly definite," Jessie said.

"It's a mystery!" Benny said, smiling.

"It sure is," Violet agreed.

When the Aldens got to the house later that day, Terry Evans was sitting on a porch step. "I just wanted to ask you a few questions," she said.

"Oh," Jessie said. "What kind of questions?"

"About the house, of course," Terry replied. "Do you know anything about the girl who used to live here . . . Celia Roth?"

"The girl who disappeared?" Benny asked eagerly.

Terry nodded.

"We don't know anything at all," Violet answered.

"This house should really be a Greenfield landmark," Ms. Evans said. "With its strange history, no one should be allowed to buy it."

"What history?" Benny asked.

"Well," Terry said, "I've heard a number of people lived here after the Roths left. But no one stayed long. For whatever reasons, they left fairly quickly. Ghosts, you know." She smiled slyly, waved, and left.

Mr. Farley, who was back in his yard, walked over to the Aldens. "Why's that woman snooping around?" he asked. "She sure asks a lot of questions."

Henry wanted to ask Mr. Farley what he and Mr. Yeats had been arguing about. But he didn't want Mr. Farley to think they'd been eavesdropping. Instead he asked, "Mr. Farley, how long did Mr. Roth stay after Celia disappeared?"

Mr. Farley thought for a minute. "Just a few months. He was mysterious. Wouldn't talk about Celia at all. He just left Greenfield."

"Ms. Evans said other people lived here," Jessie said.

Mr. Farley nodded. "Yes, a few families bought the house, lived here a short time, and then left. It's been empty now for a good twenty years. The only thing left from the Roths is an old bed, that big old desk upstairs, and some boxes of old books."

"When did Celia disappear?" Jessie asked.

Mr. Farley said, "I remember it all well. I was only ten years old, but some things you don't forget. It was the summer of 1917. August, it was. A hot day in August and, poof, she just vanished. But I know she came back . . . to the house . . . for some reason . . . or at least her ghost did."

Henry laughed. "Come on, Mr. Farley. We just don't believe that."

The Aldens went into the house and sat down on the floor.

"What do you think happened to Celia?" Jessie asked.

"Maybe she was kidnapped," Violet said.

"Or she might have drowned in the lake," Henry suggested.

"Maybe Celia ran away, just like we did," Benny said.

"Yes, Benny, but Grandfather found us," Violet said. "No one ever found Celia."

CHAPTER 5

The Mysterious Dress

Suddenly, Benny sniffed. "I smell something sweet . . . like perfume."

"I smell it, too," Jessie said.

"It's like roses," Henry said.

"It's coming from the living room," Violet said.

The children hurried into the living room. There they saw something they didn't expect. On the mantel was a vase with three fragrant yellow roses in it.

"These weren't here yesterday," Violet said, startled.

"Maybe Mr. Farley took some from his garden and put them in here," Jessie said thoughtfully.

"Maybe, but how would he have gotten in? We always lock the door when we go," Henry said. "Let's go ask him."

The Aldens went outside. Mr. Farley was still working in his yard.

"Mr. Farley," Benny called out.

Mr. Farley stopped weeding as the children approached. "Yes?" he said.

"Did you put any roses in the living room in the Roth house?" Violet asked.

Mr. Farley snorted. "Of course not. I don't grow roses, and I sure wouldn't waste money buying flowers for an empty house."

"Well, someone did," Jessie said. "Come look."

Mr. Farley followed the Aldens into the house and into the living room. He looked at the roses on the mantel. "Well, you're right. They sure are roses."

"Maybe Mrs. Carter put them here," Henry said.

"She and her husband went off early this morning," Mr. Farley said, "and they haven't come home yet."

The Aldens were silent.

"I told you there were funny things going on in this house. Now maybe you'll believe me," Mr. Farley said. "Celia used to love roses. I remember that. She grew them in her garden." Then he turned and went back to his house.

"Mr. Farley is right. There are strange things going on," Violet said.

"Violet, there are good explanations for everything," Jessie said, but she didn't sound too sure.

"I know what we should do," Henry said. "We'll go to the library in the morning and see what we can find out about the Roths from old newspapers."

"Great idea," Jessie said.

"I think we should tell Grandfather what's going on," Benny said.

"Benny is right," Violet said.

Jessie hesitated. "We don't want him to think we're just foolish kids."

Henry shook his head. "Grandfather would never think that. He knows we aren't."

At the table that night, they all ate Mrs. McGregor's delicious meal of lamb chops, baked potatoes, and string beans. Then she brought in a big bowl of cut-up fresh fruit and a plate of spice cookies. She put the bowl in front of Henry to serve. As he dished out the fruit for his family, he said, "Grandfather, there's something we want to talk to you about."

Grandfather looked concerned. "There's nothing wrong, is there?"

"It's about the Roth house," Benny said. "It's a funny house."

"Funny?" Grandfather asked.

"Well," Violet began. "Benny is right. There are funny things *in* the house and funny people *outside* the house."

Jessie said, "The things in the house can all be explained, I'm sure. Like a window shade suddenly fell on the floor. And we heard a girl singing upstairs. And roses appeared in the living room. The shade was probably blown off the window by the wind. Henry thinks the singing came from outside the house. I guess someone put the roses in the house, but who?"

Grandfather smiled. "Probably Mrs. Thaler did, to make the house look pretty."

"I never thought of her," Violet said. "But what about the funny people?"

"How are they funny?" Mr. Alden asked.

Benny said, "Well, Mr. Farley, the next-door neighbor, is always saying the house is haunted."

Violet added, "And the other neighbor, Mr. Carter, doesn't want to *have* neighbors."

Henry said, "And there's this man, an artist named Thomas Yeats, who is upset because the house will be fixed up. He's painting a picture and doesn't want the house changed."

"And there's Terry Evans. She's writing a book. *She* thinks the house should be a landmark," Jessie said.

"These people don't sound so odd to me, except maybe Mr. Farley," Grandfather said. "But he probably just has a big imagination. I think you children do, too. I suggest you forget about Mr. Farley's ghost and have fun fixing up the house. Joe and Alice will be so pleased."

"You're right, Grandfather," Jessie said. "That's just what we'll do. We all do have *big* imaginations."

But in the morning, the Aldens went to the library anyway. Ms. Gary, the librarian, smiled at them. "Can I help you?" she asked.

Jessie smiled back at her. "We wonder if you have any old Greenfield newspapers that go back to 1917?"

"We have some on microfilm. Is there anything in particular you're looking for?" Ms. Gary asked.

"Well, we'd like to read about when Celia Roth disappeared. Our cousins are buying the old Roth house," Violet said.

"That was a long time ago," Ms. Gary said.

"It was August," Benny said. "Mr. Farley told us that."

"Well, that's a help," Ms. Gary said as she left the room. "I'll be right back."

She returned soon with two rolls of microfilm. "This is the Greenfield paper from August 1917. Do you know how to use the microfilm machine?" she asked. "It's upstairs."

"I know how. We learned in school," Jessie said.

"Ours is an old machine," Ms. Gary said. "Not like the newest ones."

"So is the one in school," Jessie replied. The Aldens ran up the stairs, and Jessie put the film into the machine and started moving the film through. "I'll yell when I get to something," she said, looking at the screen.

The other children were silent while Jessie looked. After a while she shouted, "Here! Here's something."

"Let me see," Violet said. "The date is August 4th. It says, *Celia Roth is missing*."

"What else does it say?" Benny asked excitedly.

Violet read. "*Seventeen-year-old Celia Roth has vanished from her father's house. Mr. Robert Roth has refused to discuss the disappearance with reporters. The Greenfield police have questioned Mr. Roth and they also refuse to be interviewed*."

"Let me look, too," Henry said. He took Violet's place at the machine. "Here's more. On August thirty-first it says, *The Greenfield police are no longer investigating the case of Celia Roth*."

"That's funny," Jessie said. "Keep looking."

Henry looked for another five minutes. "There's nothing else," he said.

The Aldens went downstairs, returned the film to Ms. Gary, and left the library.

Benny said, "Well, we don't know anything more than we did before."

They all got on their bikes. "Let's go to the house and do some more work," Jessie said. "Before we know it, Joe and Alice will be here."

When they got to the house, Thomas Yeats was across the street. His easel was set up and he was busy working on his painting of the Roth house.

Benny waved and called out, "Hi, Mr. Yeats. Can I look at your painting?"

Mr. Yeats looked across the street at Benny. "No, you can't," he replied gruffly.

"It's probably a rotten painting anyway," Benny grumbled.

"He sure is an unfriendly man," Jessie said.

"Let's just ignore him," Violet said. "I know what needs cleaning very badly . . .

the big bathroom in the master bedroom."

"Ugh," Benny said. "I don't want to clean a bathroom."

"Okay, Benny," Henry said, "you can clean the inside of the big bedroom's windows. I'll help Jessie and Violet with the bathroom."

The Aldens carted cleanser, soap, a bucket, and rags up to the bathroom. Jessie and Violet scrubbed the sink and the tub while Henry washed down the tiles. Little by little the bathroom began to look white instead of gray.

In the bedroom, Benny sprayed window cleaner on the panes of glass and carefully wiped them with a soft rag. The sun sparkled on the panes and Benny cried out, "You should see what a good job I'm doing!"

"I'm sure you are," Violet called back to Benny. "We'll come and look."

The Aldens gathered around Benny and admired his hard work. Then Jessie pointed to a closet door. "We never looked in there."

Henry walked over and pulled open the heavy wooden door. He peered into the closet. "There are a few boxes in here."

The other children came over to him and looked into the closet, too. Violet said, "There are books in those boxes. Lots of books."

"We'll have to go through them some time," Jessie said. "That should be fun."

"Like when we cleaned up that old library," Benny said.

"Maybe there are boxes of things in the other closets," Violet said. "I'll go look in the next bedroom."

In a few minutes the children heard her cry out, "Come here! Look what's on the bed."

Benny, Henry, and Jessie ran into the next room. Violet pointed to the single bed that was against a wall and stretching into the room. What they saw surprised them even more than the roses had. There was a dress on the bed. A pale pink, long dress. The hem, neckline, and wrists were trimmed with a delicate lace. It was a beautiful dress, and the children could tell that it was very old.

"That dress wasn't here yesterday," Violet said.

"It wasn't here any day we were in this room," Henry added.

"Where do you suppose it came from?" Jessie asked.

"I'll bet it was once Celia's dress," Benny said.

"It looks like it might have been. And I'll bet this was her room," Violet said.

The Aldens were silent, each thinking about how the dress could have gotten into the room.

"I'm going to call Grandfather," Violet said. "I want him to come here and see what we see. Then he won't think we just have big imaginations."

"There's no phone in this house," Benny said. "How are you going to call him?"

"I'll go next door and ask the Carters if I can use their phone. I know they're home because I saw their car in the driveway," Violet said firmly.

"I don't know if we should bother Grandfather at work with this," Jessie said thoughtfully.

"Grandfather won't mind," Benny said. "He always tells us we should call him anytime if we need him."

Henry said, "That's true, but do we really need him to come to look at an old dress?"

"It isn't just an old dress, Henry," Violet said. "You know that. It's a *very old dress* that just suddenly appeared out of *nowhere*. I want Grandfather to see it."

"Okay," Jessie said. "Let's go and call him."

The Aldens hurried next door to the Carter's house and knocked at the door. Soon Mrs. Carter appeared. She smiled when she saw the children. "Hi. Can I do something for you?"

"We'd like to use your phone, if we could," Violet said. "I want to call my grandfather."

"I hope nothing is wrong," Mrs. Carter said, looking very curious.

"Well, I'm not sure," Violet replied. "Something very strange just happened to us."

"Do you want to tell me about it?" Mrs. Carter asked.

"First I want to call Grandfather," Violet said.

Mrs. Carter led the Aldens into the house. "There's a phone in the kitchen that you can use," she said, pointing to a room to her right.

Violet took the receiver off the kitchen wall and dialed a number. "I'd like to speak to Mr. Alden, please," she said. "This is his granddaughter Violet."

Soon Mr. Alden's voice boomed over the phone. "Violet! Are you all right? Is something wrong?"

"We're fine, Grandfather," she said.

"Don't be upset. But something just happened at the Roth house, and I'd like you to come over. A dress appeared, an old dress, out of nowhere."

Grandfather hesitated. "I'm sure there's a logical explanation, dear. But you do sound upset. I'll be with you as soon as I can drive over there."

Violet hung up. Mrs. Carter was leaning against the sink, looking very interested in Violet's conversation. The other Aldens were standing near the doorway.

"How about if I give you children some milk and cookies while you're waiting for your grandfather?" Mrs. Carter said.

"I think that's a very good idea," Benny said.

"Are you sure it isn't any trouble?" Jessie asked.

"It will be a pleasure," Mrs. Carter answered.

Just then Mr. Carter came into the kitchen. "I thought I heard a lot of strange voices," he said.

Mrs. Carter looked at him with a funny expression on her face. "It's just the Alden children. They're going to have milk and cookies while they wait for their grandfather."

"Why is *he* coming?" Mr. Carter asked. "Aren't there enough people here?"

Mrs. Carter laughed nervously. "Don't mind my husband, children. He really isn't as grumpy as he sounds."

She opened the refrigerator door and took out a large carton of milk. She filled four glasses and set them on the kitchen table. "Sit down. I'll put out some cookies, too."

The Aldens sat around the table, and Mr. Carter left the room. Mrs. Carter filled a plate with chocolate chip cookies and placed it in the center of the table. "They aren't homemade but they are still good," she said, smiling.

The Aldens drank and ate in silence. Then Benny slowly said, "Did you know Celia Roth?"

Mrs. Carter laughed. "No. She lived here way before I did. But I've certainly heard a lot about her from Mr. Farley."

"Do you believe in ghosts, Mrs. Carter?" Benny asked.

"Of course she doesn't," Henry said quickly.

CHAPTER 6

The Diary

Soon the Aldens heard a car stop in front of the Roth house. They ran to the front door and saw Mr. Alden getting out of the car.

"There's our grandfather," Jessie said to Mrs. Carter. "We have to go. Thanks for the phone and the snack."

"Any time," Mrs. Carter replied.

The children ran to their grandfather, and Violet said, "Come upstairs and see the dress I was telling you about."

They all went into the house and upstairs to the small bedroom. They looked at the bed. It was empty.

"The dress was here just a little while ago," Violet cried out. "Everyone saw it. We all did."

"She's right, Grandfather," Henry said. "It *was* here."

"We *all* saw it," Jessie added.

"It was right here on the bed?" Grandfather asked.

"Yes!" Violet said. "I can't believe it's gone."

"That is very odd," Mr. Alden said. He looked around the room thoughtfully. "There must be a good explanation. Meanwhile, I hope you children aren't nervous here."

"Of course not, Grandfather," Jessie said. "It *is* funny that the dress is gone. But there must be a real good reason."

"Something else happened," Henry said. "We found a couple of boxes of old books in a closet."

"That sounds interesting," Mr. Alden said. "Let me see them."

They walked into the master bedroom and showed Grandfather the books in the closet. He started looking through one box. "It's much too dark in this closet to see anything. I think we should take the boxes home and see what's in them. There might be something valuable."

"I'll help you carry the boxes downstairs," Henry said.

Together Henry and Mr. Alden carried the two boxes down and put them in Mr. Alden's car. "I think you children have had enough for one day. Why don't you bike home now," he said.

"I like that idea," Benny replied.

"Before we go, Grandfather. Look at the man across the street. He's the artist we told you about," Violet said.

Mr. Alden gazed at Thomas Yeats. "He seems ordinary enough to me, Violet. Just an artist painting a picture of a house."

"Not a very nice artist," Violet said. "A

grumpy one, just like Mr. Carter."

Grandfather laughed. "Well, unfortunately, everyone isn't pleasant all the time."

It took much longer for the children to bike home than for Mr. Alden to drive there. So by the time they had arrived at their house, Grandfather already had the boxes of books in the den. He also had some good news for them.

He said, "Aunt Jane called. Uncle Andy is away on business, so she's going to come and spend a few days visiting us."

Benny asked, "When will she get here? I can't wait."

Grandfather laughed. "Well, you won't have to wait too long. She'll be here in the morning. She said she would leave Elmford very early."

Violet was already busy pulling books out of the two cartons. The other children joined her and they all sat on the floor, examining them. Grandfather sat in his favorite chair reading the newspaper. He enjoyed their laughter as they found books that seemed very old and outdated.

Jessie pulled out a magazine that featured women's styles. "Look at these dresses," she cried out. "They're so funny."

"And the hats," Violet added. "Can you imagine wearing something like that now?"

Henry looked at the pictures, too. "You know, some of these dresses look just like the one that was on the bed in the Roth house."

Jessie closed the magazine and looked at the date on the cover. "This is from February 1917."

"So the dress we saw *could* have been Celia's," Violet said softly.

"*Violet!*" Jessie said. "Even if it was Celia's dress a long time ago, there's no such thing as ghosts. The dress got on the bed in some logical way."

Mrs. McGregor came to the door of the den and said, "Dinner will be ready in five minutes. You children all go upstairs and wash your hands very well. You're all dirty from those dusty old books."

In a few minutes they all sat down to a wonderful chicken dinner. The children were impatient, however, to get back to the books, which interested them all. Even Benny had found something special — a few old children's books. And Watch liked sniffing at the old books. So they ate faster than usual and decided to save their dessert until later.

They ran back into the den and continued going through the two boxes. The evening was filled with one or another of the children calling out, "Look at this one" or "Have you ever seen anything like this?" or "Look at what a car looked like then!"

Suddenly Violet called out, "I've found something wonderful!"

She held in her hands a cracked blue leather book. Printed on the cover in gold letters was *My Diary*. On the first page was written in a delicate, perfect handwriting, *This book belongs to Celia Roth*.

The Aldens all crowded around Violet and looked at the diary. "I'm not sure it's right to read it," Jessie said.

"Jessie, the diary is years and years old. Celia Roth is probably dead now. What harm is there in reading it?" Violet asked.

Jessie said firmly, "I wouldn't want anyone reading *my* diary — even seventy-five years later."

Violet turned to Mr. Alden, who was listening to the conversation. "What do *you* think, Grandfather?"

Mr. Alden said, "Well, I don't really see anything wrong in reading the diary of someone who wrote it so long ago."

Violet opened the book, and Henry said, "See if there are any entries for August, the month she disappeared."

Violet read aloud: *"August 1, 1917 . . . Dear Diary, I told Father last night that I was in love with George Collins and that we wanted to get married. I explained that since George is in the army and due to go overseas we wanted to be wed before he went. Father was very upset. He said he would never allow that. He said George and I didn't know each other well enough and that it was a foolhardy thing to do. He said he would never give his permission. I cried and cried but he refused to change his mind."*

Jessie sighed. "Isn't that romantic?"

"Read some more, Violet," Henry said.

Violet went on. "*August 3, 1917 . . . Dear Diary, I tried to talk to Father about George again, but he still won't listen to how I feel. He wants George and me to wait until the end of the war. But who knows how long it will last? George is coming over tonight and he is going to try to change Father's mind.*

"*August 4, 1917 . . . Dear Diary, George had no luck either. I am so unhappy. I don't want to disobey Father, but I want so much to marry George now.*

"*August 5, 1917 . . . Dear Diary, George and I had a long talk today. He is sure he is going to be shipped to Europe soon. What are we going to do? I never thought Father could be so stubborn. I know Father loves me and I love him. But I love George, too.*

"August 6, 1917 . . . Dear Diary, I feel much better tonight. Father seemed so calm and kind today. I am sure that if I'm patient he will come around and see my point of view. He almost always does. I'm sure everything will be fine."

Violet flicked the pages. "That's the last entry," she said.

Jessie frowned. "It seems as if Mr. Roth really didn't understand how unhappy Celia was."

Benny said, "I think it's all very mushy."

The other children laughed. Grandfather said, "Well, children, you certainly have made an interesting discovery. But now it's late. Benny, I think you should be off to bed."

Benny kissed Mr. Alden good night and started for the stairs. He smiled broadly. "Tomorrow Aunt Jane will be here."

CHAPTER 7

Aunt Jane Arrives

In the morning, the Aldens made breakfast. Jessie dipped pieces of bread into egg and milk for French toast. Benny set the table. Violet put out the maple syrup and jam, and Henry filled glasses with milk.

After the bread was browned, the children ate the tasty meal and then cleaned up the kitchen.

"Let's wait in the boxcar for Aunt Jane," Benny said.

Henry said, "Good idea. I'll tell Mrs. McGregor where we are."

Once the Aldens were in their beloved boxcar, they sat on the floor on the colorful cushions.

"You know," Jessie said, "before I went to sleep last night I kept thinking about the Roth house. I kept wondering if someone was deliberately trying to scare us away — and scare Joe and Alice away, too."

"What do you mean?" Henry asked.

"Well," Jessie went on, "maybe someone is behind the singing, and the dress, and all that . . . doing it on purpose."

"Who would want to do a thing like that?" Violet asked.

"I don't know for sure," Jessie answered, "but look at all the people who might have a reason. Mr. Carter doesn't want any neighbors. And Mr. Yeats doesn't want the house changed. And Ms. Evans thinks the house should be a landmark. Maybe one of them thinks we'll tell Joe and Alice not to buy the house."

"Yeah," Benny said, "and Mr. Farley is just plain weird."

Henry shook his head. "Jessie, no one has a key to the house but Joe and Alice, and now us. So how would someone get in? There has never been any sign of anyone breaking in."

"Henry is right," Violet said.

Jessie sighed. "I don't know."

Then Violet read to Benny while Jessie and Henry worked on a model airplane, until there was a knock at the door. Benny opened it, and there was Aunt Jane.

"It's so good to see all of you," she cried, hugging each one of them.

"We're awfully glad to see you, too," Violet said. "We have an extra pillow, so you can sit down with us."

When they all settled themselves on the pillows, Aunt Jane said, "Your grandfather tells me you've been having some mysterious adventures in Joe and Alice's new house."

"We certainly have," Violet said. And she

immediately started telling her aunt the entire story of the house and all the strange happenings. She also told her about Mr. Farley and the Carters and Thomas Yeats and Terry Evans.

"*And*," Jessie said, "we found Celia's diary yesterday."

Then they all had to tell Aunt Jane about the diary. She listened carefully and said, "There certainly has been a lot happening. I think we should go over to the house now and you can show me around."

They piled into Aunt Jane's car and rode into Greenfield. As they drove down Main Street, Violet cried out, "Look!"

"What?" Henry asked.

"It's Ms. Evans, and look at what she's carrying."

They all looked at Terry Evans, who was walking down the street. Her arms were full of yellow roses.

"Remember," Violet said, "we found three yellow roses in the living room at the Roth house. And *we* didn't put them there."

Aunt Jane laughed. "Violet, dear, anyone can buy yellow roses."

"Aunt Jane is right," Henry said.

"That's true," Violet said. "But it doesn't mean Ms. Evans *didn't* put the roses we saw into the living room."

When they got to the house, Aunt Jane went over to admire Mr. Farley's garden, as the children headed up to the porch. Benny pointed to the mailbox. "There's a letter in it," he said.

Jessie reached into the box and took out an envelope. On the front was printed THE ALDEN CHILDREN. She opened the envelope, took out a piece of paper, read it, and gasped.

"What does it say?" Henry asked.

Jessie handed the letter to Henry. He read, "*Aldens: Go home and stay home.*"

"I'll bet Mr. Carter wrote it. He said he didn't like neighbors," Benny said.

Henry said firmly, "We certainly aren't going to let whoever wrote it scare us away. Are we?"

"No!" Jessie said.

"We aren't," Benny agreed.

"I guess not," Violet said.

Henry looked back at Aunt Jane, who was coming up the front walk. "Don't mention this to Aunt Jane. She and Grandfather might not want us to come back here anymore — and then we'd never solve this mystery."

"That certainly is a beautiful garden next door," Aunt Jane said, stepping up onto the porch. "Come on, let's go in and you can give me a tour."

They all went through the house, and Aunt Jane said, "It's a lovely house. Joe and Alice will be very happy here. And you children have done a lot of cleaning. I can see that."

"But there is still more we want to do," Violet said. "We want to finish cleaning out the closets, and we haven't gone through the big desk."

"And I have a little more painting to do," Henry said.

"And I want to finish cleaning the windows," Benny added.

"Well," Aunt Jane said, "you still have time. Grandfather says Joe and Alice won't be here for another couple of weeks."

There was a knock on the door, and a telephone man came in. "I have an order for a phone to be installed here. A Mr. James Alden left it with the phone company."

"That's our grandfather," Benny said.

"Where do you want it?" the man asked.

Aunt Jane looked thoughtful. "Why don't you put it in the kitchen? Then the owners can have extensions added wherever they want them."

The telephone man went into the kitchen, and Aunt Jane and the children sat on the porch steps while he worked. Mrs. Carter saw them there and came over. The Aldens introduced her to Aunt Jane.

Mrs. Carter said, "Your nieces and nephews have certainly been busy fixing up this place. They don't even seem to be bothered by the rumors of a ghost in the house."

Aunt Jane smiled. "Of course they aren't bothered. They are sensible children and certainly don't believe in ghosts."

Just then the phone man came outside. "Well, I've hooked up the phone and it's working."

The man left and Aunt Jane asked, "Do you children want to stay here and work or not? I'm ready to go home."

Benny said, "I want to be with you, Aunt Jane."

"Me, too," the other Aldens said.

"Good," their aunt said. "We'll stop in town and have some lunch and then go home."

They ate in the Greenfield Coffee Shop and then spent the afternoon playing Monopoly and Scrabble with Aunt Jane. None of the children mentioned the nasty letter they'd received.

At the dinner table that night, Grandfather said, "I have some good news for you. Alice called this afternoon and said they are planning on moving earlier than they thought they would. They've sold their house and the new owners want to move in next week, if possible."

"Next week!" Jessie cried out. "We won't have time to finish everything."

"Well, just do the best you can," Mr. Alden said. "I know you've done a great deal already."

Henry sat silently. Then he said, "I have an idea! Suppose we go over tomorrow and stay overnight. That way we can work all day and the next morning, too, without going back and forth."

Benny looked surprised. "There's only one bed," he said.

"We'll bring sleeping bags," Jessie said.

"And food," Benny added.

Violet looked unsure. "You want to stay there *at night*?" she asked.

"Violet," Jessie said firmly, "there's nothing to be nervous about. You know there are *no ghosts* in that house."

"I forgot about the ghost," Benny said.

Grandfather looked uncertain. "I certainly don't think there are any ghosts in the house, but I'm not sure you children should stay there alone."

Jessie looked at Aunt Jane pleadingly. Aunt Jane said, "Well, James, there *are* neighbors on both sides of them. That Mrs. Carter seems like a very nice woman. If they needed anything I'm sure she would be very helpful."

"And the phone has been installed," Henry added. "So we can always call you."

Grandfather smiled. "It's hard to resist you children. I guess it's all right. But the least little thing that goes wrong, you will call me. Right?"

"Absolutely, Grandfather," Jessie said.

CHAPTER 8

The Letter

The next afternoon, the children packed up their sleeping bags, pajamas, and a change of clothes. Henry put in a flashlight, some more cleaning equipment, and a camera.

"What's the camera for?" Benny asked, sounding puzzled.

"I just thought it would be fun to take some pictures while we're working. Joe and Alice can put them in their scrapbook," Henry said.

Aunt Jane said, "I'll drive you all over to the house and pick you up in the morning."

"Can we take Watch?" Benny asked.

"That's a good idea," Henry said. "He's a good watch dog."

"What about food?" Benny asked.

"I heard that," Mrs. McGregor said. She came into the living room carrying a big picnic basket. "Everything you'll need is in here. For dinner there is a cold roast chicken, raw vegetables, potato salad, and cake. There's fresh fruit for an evening snack. Just remember to put everything in the refrigerator as soon as you get to the house."

"I'll remember that," Violet said.

"Oh," Mrs. McGregor said, "there are also two cartons of milk and a thermos of lemonade. And cold cereal and bananas for breakfast."

"They certainly won't starve." Aunt Jane laughed.

They all piled into Aunt Jane's car, and she drove to the Roth house. Watch jumped out when the door was opened and ran around the house. When Henry whistled, however, he came right back.

"You'd better keep him indoors," Aunt Jane said. "You don't want him to get lost."

"Don't worry," Benny said. "He won't go far."

"All right," Aunt Jane said. "I'll be back in the morning. If you need anything, just call home."

The children watched her car drive away and then they went inside. They got to work right away, polishing and scrubbing and making sure the house was as clean as they could make it. As they worked, they noticed the sun that had filled the house was gone. Violet looked out of a window and said, "Look at the sky! It's filled with dark clouds."

Henry looked out, too. "It's going to rain. I'll turn on the radio and see what the weather report is."

The Aldens gathered around the radio and

listened. "*A severe storm watch is now in effect*," the announcer said. "*Heavy rain and lightning are expected.*"

Benny frowned. "I don't like that."

Henry laughed. "You're not afraid of thunder and lightning."

"I know," Benny said. "But I just hope the lights don't go out."

Violet's eyes widened. "Me, too."

Jessie said quickly, "Come on, let's get dinner ready. We can open our sleeping bags and sit on them while we eat."

The Aldens all went into the kitchen and took Mrs. McGregor's feast out of the refrigerator. They put everything on paper plates and sat on the living room floor to eat their dinner.

As they were finishing, a flash of brilliant lightning filled the room, followed by a loud clap of thunder. The lights flickered and the children all exchanged worried glances.

Something banged upstairs. "What was that?" Violet asked.

"It's probably just a door that blew shut," Jessie said.

"But there are no windows open to blow it shut," Violet said.

Watch sat next to Violet, his tail beating on the floor, and he whined loudly. "Even Watch is scared," Benny said.

"There's nothing to be scared of, Benny," Henry said.

Suddenly a sweet smell filled the room. The smell of roses. "There's that smell again. Like roses. Only there are no roses here," Violet said. "Remember they died and we threw them away."

"Well, then only the smell stayed," Jessie said.

"I want to talk to Grandfather," Benny said. "I just want to say hello."

"Go ahead, Benny," Henry said, following him into the kitchen.

Benny picked up the phone. "It's not working. There's no sound at all."

Henry took the phone out of Benny's hand. He listened, frowning. "Well, I guess the storm knocked some phone lines down. I'm sure it will be fixed soon."

Henry and Benny went back into the living room. "The phone isn't working," Henry said.

Violet gasped. The lights flickered again and then a sound came from upstairs. It was the same sweet voice they had heard before, singing the same sweet song. The Aldens sat in silence, scarcely breathing. And then, after a few minutes, the singing stopped.

"It can't be a radio this time," Violet said. "And all the windows are shut."

"Well, it has to be coming from somewhere," Henry said. "And it isn't from a ghost. It's just drifting in. We'll figure out from where. Meanwhile I say we get to work! There is a lot to do upstairs."

"Upstairs?" Benny said.

"Yes," Jessie agreed. "There is *nothing* up there to be afraid of, and if we do some work, it will take your mind off of the singing."

The children walked up the stairs. Jessie said, "There's that big desk in the one room we haven't looked at."

They went into the small room that held the big desk and Henry pulled open a drawer. It was filled with pads of blank paper. The Aldens opened every drawer and emptied them of old pencils, rubber bands, a pair of glasses, and assorted odds and ends. When they reached the next drawer, Henry pulled on it but it didn't move. Jessie pulled, too, and still the drawer remained shut.

"We'll never get this open," Henry said.

"Let me try once more," Jessie insisted.

She pulled as hard as she could and finally it flew open. Jessie peered inside. "There's an envelope stuck back here!" The envelope was stuck half in the drawer and half against the back of the desk. She took the drawer out of the desk, reached inside, and pulled out the envelope.

Jessie turned it over and said softly, "Look!"

Written on the front in a delicate, perfect handwriting was the word *Father*.

"It's Celia's handwriting," Violet said. "The same handwriting that was in the diary."

"Open it, Jessie!" Benny said.

Jessie ripped open the envelope and took out one sheet of paper that had the same delicate handwriting the children now could recognize.

"What does it say?" Henry asked.

Jessie said in a soft voice, "It's dated August 10, 1917. And it says:

Dear Father:

I have tried to obey you always, but now I just can't. I love George very much and we are going to be married. I am going to his parents' home in Bromley and we will be married there in a few days.

I don't mean to hurt you. Please call me when you read this and please come to our wedding.

I am putting this letter in this drawer be-

cause I know you open it every morning to take out your reading glasses to read the morning paper. So I know you will find the letter right away.

I love you very much and will be waiting to hear from you.

Your daughter, Celia"

The Aldens were silent. Then Violet said, "The letter must have gotten stuck in the back of the drawer, and Mr. Roth never saw it."

"So he thought that Celia had disappeared and he had no idea where she could have gone," Jessie said.

"Wow!" Benny said. "That was a real mystery."

Violet's voice trembled a little. "Poor Celia. She must have waited to hear from her father and she never did. So she thought he didn't want to talk to her."

"It's so sad," Jessie said.

Just then Benny let out a big yawn. Henry smiled at him. "Let's quickly finish cleaning out this desk, then we can go to sleep," he said. "It's been a long day."

The bottom drawer opened easily. Violet looked in and said, "Look at this! It's a tape player."

She lifted it out carefully and placed it on the desk.

"There's a tape in it, too," Benny said.

Jessie rewound the tape to where it started and pushed the play button. A girl's sweet voice, singing a sad song, filled the room. "That's the singing we've been hearing," Jessie cried out.

"*It was a tape all the time*," Violet said. "Not Celia's ghost."

"There's no such thing as *ghosts*, Violet," Benny said.

"This tape recorder couldn't have belonged to the Roths. It's brand-new," Jessie pointed out. "Someone brought it here just to play this tape."

"Who would do that?" Henry asked. "Who would play this, knowing it would bother us?"

"Let's go downstairs and get into our sleeping bags," Violet said. "We can talk about it some more."

Once the children were snugly in their sleeping bags, Jessie said, "Well, someone is deliberately trying to scare us. Who?"

"It's probably the same person who brought the flowers and the dress and left the letter in the mailbox," Henry said.

By now the rain had stopped and the house was quiet. "Can we talk about this in the morning?" Benny asked. "I'm sleepy."

Henry laughed. "Sure. But there isn't that much to talk about. It has to be either Mr. Carter or Mr. Farley or Ms. Evans or Mr. Yeats."

"But how do we find out which one of them it is?" asked Violet.

"I don't know," said Henry. "Maybe we'll think of something in the morning."

CHAPTER 9

The Back Stairs

The Aldens woke up early. The storm had moved on, and sun filled the house as they ate the breakfast of cold cereal and bananas and drank the milk Mrs. McGregor had packed. They tried the phone and were happy to find it was working again.

"There isn't much more work we can do," Violet said. "Let's just clean up the kitchen."

"I want to go upstairs again and make sure everything looks neat there," Jessie said.

"We can use the back staircase," Henry added.

The children walked up the back stairs, which Henry lit with the flashlight. Halfway up, Jessie stepped on something soft, and stumbled. She bent down and picked up a gray and red sweater. "This is Mrs. Carter's," she said. "She had it on the first time we met her. Why is it here?"

"She must have been using this staircase," Henry said.

"But how did she get in?" Violet asked. "We were always so careful to lock the doors."

"Then she must have had a key," Benny said. "But why does she have it?"

"I know what we should do," Jessie said. "We'll hide outside. If we close all the windows and pull down all the shades, the Carters will think we've gone home. If they're the ones who've been trying to scare us, they'll probably come back into the house again soon."

The Aldens quickly packed their things

and rolled up their sleeping bags. Henry looked out the window and spotted a couple of large bushes at the side of the house that would be a perfect hiding place. They were big enough for the children to hide in, and from there they'd be able to see anyone who might come up the front walk or use the back door.

The children locked up the house, and walked down the front walk as if they were going home. Then one by one they sneaked into the bushes. Jessie and Benny watched the front walk, and Henry and Violet watched the back door.

"Look!" Henry finally whispered. "Mr. and Mrs. Carter are going in the back door. And they *do* have a key."

The Aldens stayed hidden and soon the Carters came out of the house carrying the tape player and a lacy pink dress.

"That's the dress that was on the bed!" Violet said. "And the tape player."

The children watched the Carters go back into their own house. "We have to tell

Grandfather and Aunt Jane about this," Henry said. "Come on, let's call home."

The Aldens went back into the house and phoned their grandfather. Jessie quickly told him what had happened and he said, "Just stay in the house. Aunt Jane and I will drive right over. Don't talk to anyone. Just stay there."

"What are we going to do until Grandfather gets here?" Benny asked.

"I know," Violet said. "Let's take some pictures with the camera you brought, Henry."

They tried to forget about the Carters while they took pictures of each other in funny poses. Finally, they heard a car pull up to the house. They ran out to Grandfather and Aunt Jane.

Grandfather looked very serious. "I think we have to talk to the Carters about what you saw and get an explanation from them."

They walked up to the Carters' front door and rang the bell. Mr. Carter answered, looking, as usual, very unfriendly. "Yes?" he said.

"We'd like to come in and talk to you and your wife about something very important," Grandfather said.

"We don't want any visitors," Mr. Carter said.

Then Mrs. Carter appeared behind her husband at the door. "What's going on?" she asked.

"We'd just like a few minutes with you and your husband," Grandfather said.

Mrs. Carter looked at Mr. Alden's serious, unsmiling face and her own face turned pale. She glanced at her husband and then said to the Aldens, "Come in."

They all went into the Carters' living room. "Won't you sit down?" she said to Mr. Alden and Aunt Jane.

They sat and the children stood near them. "Why don't you tell the Carters what has been happening and what you saw," Grandfather said to Jessie.

Jessie began. "All sorts of strange things

have been happening in the Roth house. We found roses we didn't put there. An old dress was on the bed one day — and then it disappeared. A threatening note was in the mailbox. And there was this voice . . . the voice of a girl singing a song. Last night we found a tape player with a tape of the girl's voice. And this morning, Mrs. Carter, we found your sweater on the back stairway. And then . . ." Jessie hesitated, "we saw you and your husband unlocking the back door and going into the house. You came out carrying the tape player and the dress."

Mrs. Carter gasped.

Grandfather said, "Since you knew where the tape player and the dress were, you must have put them there. You have been deliberately trying to frighten my grandchildren. Why? I don't like people upsetting my family."

Mrs. Carter began to weep softly. "I'm so sorry," she said. "I knew this wasn't right."

"I think you'd better explain," Mr. Alden said.

Mr. Carter, now as pale as his wife, began to talk. "It was the house. We had wanted to buy the Roth house and the land for a long time. But we never had enough money to do so. We thought if we made sure the house stayed empty long enough, we would manage to save the money to buy it."

Mrs. Carter took up the story. "When we heard that Joe and Alice Alden had bought the house, we thought that if they could be made to believe the house was haunted, they wouldn't move in. Then we would have a chance to buy the house someday. So we did all the things Jessie mentioned. But I guess the children were smarter than we were."

"What you did wasn't very nice," Benny said. "I really was scared."

"I'm sorry, Benny. I know what we did was wrong," Mrs. Carter said.

"Where did you get a key to the house from?" Violet asked.

"Once the real estate agent gave us a key to let some people in to see the house, on a day she couldn't show it herself. We just made a duplicate of the key."

"The dress, and the roses . . . you did all that?" Violet asked.

"Yes," Mrs. Carter said. "I found that dress in an antique clothing store, and it seemed like the kind of thing Celia might have worn. Mr. Farley had told us about the Roth's beautiful rose garden, so the roses seemed to make sense, too."

"And the singing?" Benny asked directly.

"We used the back stairs to turn on the tape recorder," Mr. Carter explained.

"But *other* people thought the house was haunted," Henry said.

"We started the rumor about the house and Celia's singing years ago," Mr. Carter said. "It worked with some people, like Mr. Farley. And even some people who bought the house didn't stay very long. They just thought that every funny sound that you normally hear in an old house came from a ghost. We were successful for a long time. Until you children came to the house," Mr. Carter said.

"We are sorry. Really. And we do hope your cousins will be very happy here. We really do," Mrs. Carter said.

"I agree with my wife," Mr. Carter said. "I want them to be happy, too. We know what we did was wrong, and I hope we can make it up to you all. If your cousins ever need anything, I hope they'll call on us."

"We accept your apologies," Violet said generously. "There was no real harm done."

The Aldens got into Grandfather's station wagon and they rode home. Jessie was frowning. "What about Celia? Where do you suppose she went? And do you think she is still alive?"

"She would be a very old lady," Aunt Jane said.

"We can't just forget about her," said Violet.

CHAPTER 10

Where is Celia?

After dinner that night, the family gathered in the den. Henry said, "How can we go about trying to find out more about Celia? Even Mr. Farley doesn't know — and he was her neighbor."

"Well, in her letter to her father she said she was going to Bromley to stay with George's parents. Maybe she's still there," Jessie said.

"But she got married. Her name wouldn't be Roth," Henry added.

Aunt Jane was thoughtful. "It doesn't seem likely that she would still be in Bromley after all these years."

"Wait a minute!" Jessie said. She ran over to the bookcase and took Celia's diary from a shelf. She ruffled through it until she came to the page was looking for. "Celia says here: *I told Father last night that I was in love with George Collins.* So Collins would have been her last name if she married George."

"You could try asking information if there's someone by the name of Celia or George Collins living in Bromley," Grandfather suggested. "People in this part of the state often stay in the same town for a lifetime."

Jessie went to the telephone and got information for Bromley. She asked, "Is there a listing for George Collins?"

The operator answered, "I'm sorry we have no one by that name."

"What about the name Celia Collins?" Jessie asked.

There was silence and then the operator returned. "Yes, I have a listing for a Celia Collins. The number is 555-3111."

"I can't believe it," Jessie said. "There *is* a Celia Collins in Bromley."

"Well, why don't you call her?" Benny asked.

Grandfather looked thoughtful. "We must all remember that Mrs. Collins is an old lady. You can't just tell her about her letter on the phone. If you want to call her, Jessie, you have to be careful how you tell the story of what has happened."

"I know, Grandfather," Jessie said. "But I *have* to call her."

Jessie went to the phone and dialed the number she had been given. She waited with her heart beating rapidly as the number rang. Then a voice answered and Jessie said, "I'd like to speak to Mrs. George Collins, please."

A sweet, strong voice said clearly, "This is she."

Jessie quickly told Celia about how they

had become connected with the old Roth house. "Well," Celia Collins said, "I lived there a long time ago."

"We know," Jessie said. "Mrs. Collins, could we come to see you? We have some things we found in the house that I think you would want. I'm sure that my grandfather would drive me and my sister and brothers over to see you. I know that Bromley is not too far from Greenfield. We wouldn't stay too long."

"What kind of things did you find?" Celia asked. Her voice sounded sad.

"I think we should bring them to you," Jessie said.

Mrs. Collins hesitated. Then she said, "All right. Can you come at eleven tomorrow morning?"

The next morning at eleven on the dot the Aldens were seated in Celia Collins's living room. Mrs. Collins was a beautiful woman with short white hair. Her eyes sparkled and her voice was firm.

"Now, you must tell me why you came here," she said.

Violet held out the diary. "We found this in an old box of books."

Mrs. Collins gasped. "My goodness! That diary goes back a long time. It was filled with all the thoughts of a seventeen-year-old. Some not very happy, I recall."

Henry cleared his throat and said, "We found something else. We found this letter jammed in the back of a drawer in a big old desk. The envelope had never been opened because it had gotten stuck in the back of the desk drawer."

Celia Collins's eyes opened wide. "My father never found the letter. Is that what you mean?"

"That's right," Jessie said. "We opened the letter. I hope you don't mind. So, you see, your father never knew where you went."

Tears came to the old lady's eyes. "I never heard from him, so I just thought he didn't want to talk to me. That he was so angry that he was disowning me. It never occurred to me that he hadn't read the letter. I waited and waited to hear from him. Then, after a number of months, I called him. But he had sold the house, and no one knew where he had gone. He was just lost to me."

"You married your George, didn't you?" Violet asked softly.

Celia Collins laughed. "Oh, yes. We married before he went overseas. When he came back, we settled here in Bromley and had three children. He died about ten years ago. My daughter lives just down the block, and I have a housekeeper who lives in this house with me. I was always sad about father, but George and I had a good life together."

Benny said, "Now you know your father wasn't mad at you. He just didn't know where you were."

"That makes me feel much better," Mrs. Collins said. She smiled at the children. "You have made me very happy, and I am delighted to have my diary back."

Grandfather stood up. "We have taken enough of your time. We should leave now."

Mrs. Collins took Violet's hand. "Will all you children come and visit and tell me more about the house?"

"If you'd like," Jessie said. "Someday maybe Grandfather will bring you to your old home so you can see it again."

"That would be my pleasure," Grandfather said.

Mrs. Collins stood and walked to the door with the Aldens. "Someday I will call you, and my housekeeper can drive me to the old house. I would like to see it again and to meet your cousins."

She kissed each of the children and shook Grandfather's hand. "I can't thank you enough for giving me back my father."

The Aldens got into Grandfather's car and rode in silence for a while. Then Jessie said, "I'm so glad we found Celia."

One month later, on a warm Sunday afternoon, there was a party going on at the old Roth house. Joe and Alice were having a housewarming party. There were platters of food and cookies and cakes on the dining room table. The living room was filled with flowers, and the house was filled with people.

All the Aldens were there and Aunt Jane and Uncle Andy. Joe and Alice had also invited Mr. Farley, Ms. Evans, Thomas Yeats, and even the Carters. The Carters, who felt so sorry that they had tried to keep Joe and Alice from moving in, had become perfect neighbors. They were helpful and welcoming. But the person whom everyone was waiting for was Celia Roth Collins. She had been invited and had said that her housekeeper would drive her over.

The moment came, and Celia Collins walked into the house she had not been in for decades. Alice ran to the door to welcome her and led her into the living room. As Mrs. Collins looked around, tears came to her eyes. "The house looks beautiful," she said to Alice.

Alice said, "Let me introduce you to everyone. You know the Aldens. And this is the children's aunt and uncle." Then she reached Mr. Farley. He looked at Celia and asked, "Do you remember me at all?"

Celia Collins stared at him. "Well, it's been a long, long time but you do look a little like a boy who lived next door to me. He was a real imp. His name was Charlie Farley."

Mr. Farley smiled broadly. "That was me! You know, Mrs. Collins, I had a real crush on you when I was a boy."

Mrs. Collins smiled, too. "I knew that, Charlie."

Mr. Farley looked thoughtful. "I think that was why I wanted to believe your ghost was still in the house. Just so I could pretend you were still here."

Alice took Celia over to Mr. Yeats. "Mr. Yeats is painting a picture of the house," she said.

"Yes, I wanted the house not to change so I could finish the painting. When the children started fixing the place up, I was so angry. I was afraid all my work would be wasted. I even asked Mr. Farley to keep an eye on the children for me — let me know what they were up to. He refused, and rightly so. Anyway, I did finish the painting."

"Perhaps," Mrs. Collins said, "you would sell it to me."

Mr. Yeats bowed slightly. "Madam, it would be a pleasure if you would let me give the painting to you as a gift."

"I would love that," Mrs. Collins replied.

The last one Alice introduced Celia to was Terry Evans. "Ms. Evans is writing a history of Greenfield."

"Yes," Ms. Evans said, "and this house will have a chapter all to itself. I wanted it to become a landmark but Joe and Alice have fixed it up so beautifully. It is as well cared for as if it were a landmark."

Everybody sat down and Celia Collins sighed. "Everything would be perfect if I just knew what happened to my father."

Ms. Evans jumped up. "I know that. I have been doing research on the families that lived in this house."

Mrs. Collins looked startled. "What happened to him?"

Ms. Evans walked over to Celia and sat down on the sofa next to her. "What I discovered is that he moved to Boston a few months after you disappeared. He tried in many ways to find you. He finally put an ad in a Boston paper, hoping you might see it. I wrote it out and brought a copy of it for you."

Celia's hand trembled as she reached for it. Then she dropped her hand and said to Ms. Evans, "I think you had better read it to me."

Ms. Evans cleared her throat and read: "*For Celia Roth, my daughter: I know that you must have married George Collins and that is why you left home. I was wrong to try to stop you from marrying George. He is a nice young man and you deserve to be happy with him. Please write to me at the box number below if you see this ad. If I don't hear from you I will know you never read this paper. I know that you love me, as I love you, and would reply if you could. Your loving father, Robert Roth.*"

There was a silence in the room after Ms. Evans stopped reading. Then Mr. Alden said, "So now you know, Mrs. Collins, that your father forgave you and knew that you loved him."

"I am so glad," Mrs. Collins said, wiping the tears from her eyes. "I will always be grateful to all of you," she said, looking around the room.

"Can we eat now?" Benny asked.

Everyone laughed and Alice said, "There's a lot of food in the dining room. Benny is right. It's time to eat."

Everyone walked into the dining room and filled their plates. Mrs. Collins's housekeeper fixed a plate for the old woman, who remained seated in the living room. The housekeeper looked at the Alden children and said, "I don't think you can know how happy you have made Mrs. Collins. Now she can stop worrying about what happened between her and her father."

Back in the living room, they all ate the wonderful food Alice and Joe had prepared. Benny sat on the floor next to Mrs. Collins and said, "Would you come and visit *us* sometime? I'd like to show you our boxcar. You know *we* ran away once, too."

Mrs. Collins smiled. "Benny, I would love to visit you and to hear about your adventures."

"We've had lots of them," Violet said. "But you know, I think this one was the best."

THE MYSTERY OF THE MUMMY'S CURSE

created by
GERTRUDE CHANDLER WARNER

Illustrated by Hodges Soileau

ALBERT WHITMAN & Company
Morton Grove, Illinois

The Mystery of the Mummy's Curse
created by Gertrude Chandler Warner;
illustrated by Charles Tang.

ISBN 978-0-8075-5504-0

Contents

CHAPTER 1

A Secret at the Museum

"Wow, look over there! Is that a T-rex?" Six-year-old Benny Alden was pointing toward a giant skull with long, pointed teeth.

"Yes, Benny, I think it is," said his twelve-year-old sister, Jessie.

"Cool," said their sister Violet, who was ten. She came over for a closer look.

"And look at this triceratops skull," said Henry, their fourteen-year-old brother. He pointed to another skull with horns coming out of the top.

The children were visiting the Dinosaur Room at the Greenfield Museum. "I always loved this room when I was a kid," said their grandfather, James Alden.

The children had lived with their grandfather ever since their parents died. At first, afraid that he would be mean to them, the children had run away. They had lived in an old boxcar they'd found in the woods. But once they met their grandfather, they found that he was a kind man, and they came to live in his large house. They had been happy there ever since. Grandfather had even moved the boxcar to their backyard, so the children could play in it. And today they were visiting the local museum.

When the Aldens had seen all the dinosaur bones, Grandfather asked what they would like to do next.

"Have lunch!" cried Benny.

"We should have guessed," said Jessie. "It's been at least an hour since breakfast."

Everyone laughed. They knew Benny was always hungry.

"Maybe soon, Benny," Grandfather said. "But first there's someone I'd like you to meet." He led them down the hall to a door that read, MUSEUM CURATOR.

"Come in," called a voice inside, after they knocked.

Grandfather pushed open the door to reveal a small office where a dark-haired man was sitting behind a desk. The man was tall and thin with a friendly smile on his face. He stood up when he saw the Aldens and came over to say hello.

"James Alden!" the man said, reaching out to shake Grandfather's hand. "My father told me you still lived in Greenfield."

"It's good to see you, Pete," Mr. Alden said. "Children, this is Peter Miller. I've known him since he was born. His father is an old friend of mine. When he told me Pete had come to the museum to work as the curator, I had to stop by and say hello."

"And these must be your grandchildren," said Mr. Miller. "Don't tell me — the tall one is Henry, Jessie is over here, Violet has the purple shirt on, and this must be Benny."

Benny grinned. "You got it!"

"Would you like to join us for some lunch, Mr. Miller?" Henry asked.

"That sounds great," Pete said. "But please don't call me 'Mr. Miller.' I'm Pete."

"When did you become the curator here?" Grandfather asked as they walked down the hallway to the museum café.

"And what is a cur — what's that word again?" Benny asked.

"A cu-ra-tor," Pete said slowly. "It's the person at the museum who puts together the exhibits."

"Which exhibits did you put together?" asked Jessie.

"I'm working on my first one," Pete said. "It's very exciting."

"What's it about?" Violet asked.

Before Pete could answer, Benny called out, "Hey, look! A mummy!" Everyone turned to see where Benny was pointing. On the wall was a poster of an Egyptian mummy.

"That answers Violet's question," Pete said. "That poster is for our new exhibit about ancient Egypt. It's called 'Enter the Mummy's Tomb.' "

"Will there really be a mummy?" Benny wanted to know.

"You bet," Pete said as they reached the café. "Let's get some lunch and I'll tell you all about it."

A few minutes later, Pete and the Aldens sat down to eat. The children had chosen sandwiches and fruit, and the two men were having soup.

But for once, Benny wasn't interested in food. "Please tell us about the mummy," he begged Pete.

Pete began speaking in a low voice. "The director of the museum wants to keep the details of the exhibit a secret," he explained. "But I don't think anyone will hear me."

"Why are you keeping it a secret?" Jessie asked quietly.

"Well, it's not really a secret," Pete said. "We've announced the exhibit in the newspapers and put up posters around town. But this is the biggest exhibit ever to come to the Greenfield Museum. We want to make sure we've got it all set up perfectly before we let out any details."

"You must know a lot about Egypt if you made an exhibit about it," Benny said.

"Actually, the exhibit was put together by the Egyptian Museum," Pete said. "We're renting it from them. Museums often share exhibits. We've also hired an expert on Egypt to help set it up."

Pete paused to eat a spoonful of his soup. Henry looked around and noticed that a young woman sitting near them had stopped eating her lunch and was watching them closely. Henry wondered why.

"Do you know what a mummy is?" Pete asked Benny.

"It's a dead person wrapped in bandages, right?" Benny said.

"That's about right," Pete said. "In ancient Egypt, they believed that when a person died they would still need their body. So they figured out a way to preserve it. They did such a good job that some mummies have lasted for thousands of years."

"Wow, that's old!" Benny said in an awed voice.

"Some mummies, especially the mummies of kings, are decorated with beautiful masks and fancy painted coffins. Some have gold and jewels on them. But our mummy isn't quite that fancy. Our exhibit will also show lots of things Egyptian people made and used thousands of years ago."

Henry was very interested in the exhibit. But he couldn't help thinking that someone else seemed to be, too. The woman sitting nearby was still watching them. She had finished eating, but she continued to sit at her table looking toward the Aldens. Henry wondered if she could hear what they were saying.

Then Henry noticed something strange.

The woman had her hands under the table. She seemed to be holding something in her lap. Henry couldn't see what it was. Why would she be hiding something under the table?

When they'd all finished their lunches, Pete said, "I'd better get back to my office."

"When did you say the exhibit opened?" Jessie asked.

"In two weeks," Pete said, standing up.

"I don't know if I can wait that long!" cried Benny.

Pete smiled and his eyes sparkled. In a hushed voice he said, "The mummy is being delivered this afternoon. Would you like to see it?"

Without a moment's pause, all four children cried, "Yes!"

Pete and Grandfather laughed. "I have to get back to my office," Grandfather said, "but the kids can walk home later without me."

"Then let's go," Pete said.

As the children said good-bye to Grandfather and left with Pete, Henry looked back at the young woman sitting near them. For the first time, she noticed Henry looking at her. She quickly stuffed whatever she was holding into a large, orange bag at her feet. Pete had said the details of the exhibit were supposed to be a secret. Had the woman overheard? Had she been listening to their conversation? And what had she put into her bag?

As Pete led the Aldens back down the hall, a voice called out, "Pete?"

Pete turned and stepped into the office next to his. "Yes, Reginald?" he said, motioning for the children to follow him.

Sitting behind a desk was a man about Grandfather's age. Behind him were a large Egyptian painting and a bookcase. Crowded in with the books were Egyptian pots and sculptures.

"Has the mummy arrived?" the man asked.

"I was just going to check now," Pete said. "These are the grandchildren of my father's good friend." Then he turned to the Aldens. "This is the director of the museum, Dr. Reginald Snood."

Pete turned back to Dr. Snood, who was putting papers into his briefcase. "I'm bringing the kids to see the mummy, if you'd like to join us. . . ."

Dr. Snood didn't seem to hear what Pete had said. He seemed to be deep in thought for a moment. Then he shook his head and seemed to see the Aldens for the first time. "I hope these children know not to touch anything," Dr. Snood said. "In my opinion, children don't belong in museums."

"They're very well behaved," Pete assured him.

"We're very excited to 'Enter the Mummy's Tomb,' " Jessie said.

"I just hope we haven't taken on more than we can handle with that exhibit," Dr. Snood said, snapping his briefcase shut and standing up.

"It looks like you're interested in Egypt," Henry said, motioning toward the artwork all around them.

"Dr. Snood is one of the world's leading Egyptologists," Pete told them. "That means he's an expert on ancient Egypt. He collects all kinds of—"

"That was years ago," Dr. Snood said, cutting Pete off, "before I became the director here. Now I have a museum to run. I have to make sure we don't waste all our time and money on one exhibit."

"This was expensive, but it will be such a hit," Pete insisted. "Sam Dickerson, the Egyptologist we've hired, will handle all the details."

"We're paying Dr. Dickerson too much," Dr. Snood said sharply. "We should have let the Carson City Museum have this exhibit."

Pete took a deep breath. "Well, anyway, as I mentioned before, we're expecting the mummy to be delivered soon. Would you like to come see it?"

A strange look passed over Dr. Snood's

face again. Then he seemed to change his mind about something. "No, I can't . . ." he said. "I have . . . a meeting. This is a very busy week." And he quickly left the office.

The Aldens looked at each other. Why had Dr. Snood left so quickly?

After a moment, Benny said quietly, "I don't think he likes us."

Pete laughed. "He takes a little getting used to. He has a very big job, running the museum. He has to make sure the museum has enough money to pay for all the exhibits and the people who work here."

They walked slowly out of Dr. Snood's office and headed down the hall.

"What did he mean about the Carson City Museum?" Henry asked.

"When the Egyptian Museum offered to rent out this exhibit, the Carson City Museum wanted it," Pete told the children. "But the Egyptian Museum decided to send it here instead. The director of the Carson City Museum was very upset."

"I didn't know museums fight over their exhibits," said Jessie.

"Sometimes they do," Pete said. He looked at his watch. "Come on, we've got a mummy to meet."

Pete led the children upstairs and down a long hallway to a room filled with tables and cardboard boxes. There was a desk in one corner with a computer on it and several neat stacks of papers and notecards. "This is the prep or 'preparation' room," Pete said.

At the back of the room were two large crates. Next to the crates stood two women. One was tall with lots of curly red hair. The other woman was short and blond.

"Dr. Dickerson," Pete said, walking to the back of the room and putting out his hand to the tall, redheaded woman.

"But, but — I thought you said *Sam* Dickerson," Benny said.

Dr. Dickerson threw back her head and laughed loudly. "That happens all the time. My real name is Samantha. But people call me Sam."

"I hope you don't mind my bringing some mummy hunters along," Pete said.

"Not at all," Dr. Dickerson said. The children were glad to see that she was much friendlier than Dr. Snood. "This is my assistant, Tina," she said, motioning to the blond woman beside her. Then she turned back to Pete. "It's here!" she said with a big smile on her face. She looked as excited as the children.

"Are there two mummies?" Benny asked.

"No—one crate holds the mummy, and the other holds its coffin," Dr. Dickerson said. "They're packed very carefully and shipped separately so they won't get damaged. Later, we'll unpack the mummy and put it into its coffin. For now, we've just removed the tops of the crates so we could make sure everything is in one piece." She turned to Pete. "Do you have a stepladder so we can get a look inside?"

Pete went out to a closet in the hall and came back a moment later with a stepladder, which he placed beside one of the crates. Dr. Dickerson climbed up and carefully removed several large pieces of foam rubber that had fit snugly into place over the top of the mummy. At last, she peered down into the crate, and a broad smile spread across her face.

"There he is," Dr. Dickerson said. "Our mummy."

After a moment, she stepped down and Pete climbed up to take a look. "Come on over and see," he said to the Aldens.

Pete stepped down. One at a time, the Aldens climbed up the stepladder and peered into the crate. Inside, they saw what looked like a person lying down, completely covered in cloth bandages. But the person had no face. Where the face should have been, there were just bandages, giving it a strange, creepy look.

"Wow!" said Benny. He couldn't believe there was really a dead body inside. He felt a chill run up his spine.

Henry was the last of the children to look into the crate. He stepped down and Tina stepped up in his place. "Oh, look at that," she said, peering into the crate. But as she shifted her feet on the top of the stepladder, she suddenly fell. "Ow!" she cried out as she landed on the floor.

Everyone rushed over. Dr. Dickerson knelt on the floor beside Tina. "What happened?" she asked, helping Tina to sit up. "Are you hurt?"

Tina grimaced in pain. "My ankle," she said, gritting her teeth. "I think I twisted it."

Dr. Dickerson and Pete looked at Tina's ankle. It was turning pink and beginning to swell. As Pete gently touched her ankle, Tina winced in pain.

"We'd better put ice on that to stop the swelling," Jessie suggested. "I'll run down to the café and get some."

"That would be great," Dr. Dickerson said.

"Yes, thank you," Tina said, her voice filled with pain.

Jessie came back a moment later with the ice. Tina held it on her ankle for several minutes. But her pain did not let up.

"I think we'd better take Tina over to the

hospital," Dr. Dickerson said. "We should get some X rays and see if anything's broken."

Dr. Dickerson drove Tina to the hospital, promising to call as soon as they knew how bad Tina's ankle was.

Pete and the Aldens waited in the prep room. "How would you guys like to see some of the other pieces in the exhibit?" Pete asked, trying to cheer everyone up.

"That would be great," Jessie said, speaking for all of them.

Pete led them over to one of the tables where some things had been unpacked from their boxes and arranged in neat rows. Next to each item was a small card with information printed on it. "These statues show what life was like in ancient Egypt." There was a woman carrying a basket on her head, and a man holding a pitcher. Some of the statues were part human and part animal. "That's how the ancient Egyptians portrayed their gods," Pete explained.

On another table were statues carved

from gray limestone, white alabaster, and yellow jasper. Some were made of clay or wood and were painted in bright colors. There were animal sculptures in gold and silver and bronze. There were also cups and pots, necklaces and bracelets.

"The Egyptians thought that after you died, in the 'afterlife,' you'd need everything you used when you were alive," Pete said. "So they buried their dead with plates, clothes, jewelry, and sometimes even chariots."

"Those two gold cats are beautiful," Violet said.

"I like the funny monkey," said Benny, pointing to a statue of a baboon.

"Over here we have instruments," Pete said, pointing to a wooden flute decorated with gold. "The Egyptians loved to sing, dance, and make music."

"What did children play back then?" Benny asked.

"Well, they didn't have video games or TV," said Pete. "But I think some of their toys will look familiar to you."

"Really?" asked Benny.

Pete pointed to the end of the table.

"Those look like balls," Henry said.

"That's right," said Pete. "Balls, marbles, spinning tops. Imagine — these toys were used thousands of years ago."

"Here's a doll that belonged to a little girl in ancient Egypt," Pete continued. The doll's body was made from a flat board decorated with patterns, and her hair was strung with clay beads. "It looks different from dolls today, but I'm sure the girl who owned it loved it just as much."

Just then the phone rang.

Pete picked up the receiver. "Hello? Yes, Sam. How is she?"

The Aldens watched as Pete's face darkened. "Oh, that's terrible," he said. "I'll see you when you get back."

Pete hung up the phone and turned to the children. "Tina's ankle is broken. She'll have to stay off it for several weeks."

"That's awful!" Violet said.

"Yes, poor Tina," Pete said. "And without

her help, how will we get this exhibit ready in time?"

"She had just looked at the mummy when she fell," said Benny.

Pete frowned. "Maybe it's the mummy's curse," he said.

CHAPTER 2

The Mummy's Curse

"What's the mummy's curse?" Jessie asked.

"Some people believe mummies should not be removed from where they were buried," said Pete. "They believe mummies carry evil spells to punish anyone who disturbs them. *That's* the mummy's curse."

"Really?" Benny asked, his eyes wide.

"A long time ago, when scientists were digging up a mummy, if someone died or got hurt or something else bad happened, people would say it was because of the curse," Pete went on.

"Is there really such a thing?" Violet asked.

"What do you think?" Pete said.

"No. If something bad happened it was just a coincidence," Henry said firmly.

"That's right," Pete said. "There's no such thing as ghosts or magic spells. And there's no such thing as a mummy's curse."

Still, Benny's eyes were wide. "But Tina fell *right after* she looked at the mummy," he said.

"I was just joking before," Pete said kindly. "It was an unfortunate accident, but it wasn't the mummy's fault."

But Benny didn't look as if he believed that. He backed away from the crate holding the mummy. He was afraid he might fall and get hurt, too.

The phone rang again. "Hello?" Pete said, picking up the receiver. "Yes, Reginald, that's right." The Aldens watched as Pete listened to what Dr. Snood was saying. He did not look happy.

"No, it's not a room we normally use," Pete said, "But — "

Again he was silent as Dr. Snood spoke. The children wondered what he was saying.

"All right," Pete said. "I'll see what I can figure out." Then he hung up the phone and sighed heavily.

"Is something wrong?" Violet asked gently.

"Well, if there were a mummy's curse, I'd say it's struck again," Pete said.

"What do you mean?" Benny asked. He sounded nervous.

Pete smiled at Benny's worried look. "Don't worry, Benny. It's not that bad." He patted Benny on the shoulder. "The exhibit was going to be in a hall we don't usually use. That was Dr. Snood on the phone. He said the cleaning crew is too busy to clean the extra room. And there's no money left in the budget to hire an extra crew. Without Tina *and* without the cleaning crew, we'll never get the exhibit ready in time." He sighed again.

"I have an idea," Jessie said.

"You do?" Pete asked, peering wearily over his fingers.

"We could help you," she said.

Pete sat up and smiled. "That's nice, but this is a big job. I'm not really sure you'd be able to help us get our exhibit ready in time."

"But there are lots of things we could do," Jessie said. "We're great cleaners. We could do the work you needed the cleaning crew to do. And we'll do it for free."

"Yeah," said Henry, getting excited. "And we can carry boxes and help Dr. Dickerson. Whatever needs to be done."

Pete was looking thoughtful.

"Why don't you call our grandfather and ask him," Henry suggested.

Pete picked up the telephone, and a few minutes later it was decided. The Aldens had a job. "You start first thing tomorrow," Pete said.

"Great," said Jessie. "We'll be back tomorrow morning, bright and early!"

As they headed out, the children stopped

in the prep room to pick up their jackets, which they'd left there.

While Henry, Jessie, and Violet put on their jackets, Benny turned to look at the two huge crates that were still at the end of the room. He couldn't resist stealing one last peek at the mummy. Benny walked over, got up on the stepladder, and peered down into the crate. The mummy was lying there, just as it had been before. Its blank face pointed up at the ceiling as if it were waiting for something.

Benny thought about the mummy's curse. The room seemed too quiet. He looked up and realized the others had left without him. Suddenly, he felt lonely and a little bit scared. He quickly got down from the stepladder.

"Hey, you guys, wait for me!" he called, running to catch up.

As they were leaving the building, Henry noticed a familiar face in the lobby. It was the woman he'd seen at lunch.

This time, the woman walked right up to

THIS SIDE
UP

them and introduced herself. "Hi, I'm Lori Paulson. I saw you guys in the café."

"Yes, we were there," Jessie said, surprised to be recognized by a stranger.

"So what have you been doing here all afternoon?" Ms. Paulson asked.

"We got to see the — " Benny began, but Jessie interrupted him.

"What my little brother was starting to say was, we just love this museum. We've been exploring."

"And we got to see the — " Benny began again.

This time, Henry grabbed Benny's arm and pulled him off to the side. "Remember, Pete said the new exhibit is supposed to be a secret," he whispered.

Meanwhile, Jessie was talking to Ms. Paulson. "We're the Aldens. I'm Jessie and this is my sister Violet. Those are my brothers, Henry and Benny."

"It's nice to meet you," Ms. Paulson said.

"What have *you* been doing here all afternoon, Ms. Paulson?" Jessie asked.

"Call me Lori," she said. "I've been . . .

Oh, I just love the museum, too." She smiled, and for a moment Jessie thought she looked uncomfortable. "I come here all the time."

Now Benny remembered not to talk about the mummy. He asked Lori, "Don't you love the dinosaurs?"

"I didn't know they had dinosaurs here," Lori said.

"Not real dinosaurs, of course," Benny said. "But they've got a bunch of skulls and bones in that big room at the back."

"Thanks for telling me," Lori said. "I'll have to check that out."

Jessie looked at her watch. Their housekeeper, Mrs. McGregor, would be putting dinner on the table soon. "I'm sorry, but we've got to be going."

"Oh, um . . ." Lori seemed to want to ask the children something. Finally, she said, "Did I see you talking to the curator at lunch?"

"Yes, Pete Miller is a friend of our grandfather's," Henry said.

Lori's face lit up. "Did he mention anything about the new Egyptian exhibit?"

The Aldens all looked at each other, not sure what to say. They didn't want to lie, but they also knew they weren't supposed to talk about the exhibit.

"He just told us that it was opening in a couple of weeks," Henry said at last.

"What's going to be in the exhibit?" Lori asked. "Will there be a mummy?"

"We've got to go," Jessie said, pointing to her watch. "Sorry."

"But—" Lori began, but the Aldens quickly headed off before she could ask any more questions.

As the Aldens walked down the front steps of the museum, Henry turned to the others. "She was in the cafeteria when we were having lunch. She kept staring at us the whole time."

"I wonder why she's so curious about the new exhibit," Jessie added.

"Maybe she just likes mummies," Benny said. "Like me."

"I get the feeling there's something more to it," Henry said. "You should have seen how she was watching us during lunch. And there's something else strange about her."

"What?" asked Violet.

"She says she comes here all the time. So how come she's never seen the dinosaur bones?" Henry said.

"That is pretty strange," Jessie agreed.

"I think maybe Lori Paulson isn't telling us the truth," Henry said.

"But why would she lie?" Violet asked.

"I bet it has something to do with the Egyptian exhibit she's so curious about," said Jessie.

"Well, I don't know about you guys, but I'm too hungry to worry about Lori Paulson," Benny said. "Let's go home for dinner!"

The next day, the Aldens arrived before the museum opened, ready to work. The building was quiet and almost empty. As they walked down the long, dark hallway to the prep room for the Egyptian exhibit, their footsteps echoed on the hard floor.

A light was shining under the door of the prep room. When the Aldens pushed the door open, they were surprised to see not Sam or Pete, but Dr. Snood. He was standing up on the stepladder, peering down into the mummy's crate. He seemed to be deep in thought.

"Hello, Dr. Snood," Jessie said.

Dr. Snood looked up suddenly. He seemed startled, as if he'd been caught doing something he shouldn't. He quickly stepped down from the stepladder. "I was just . . ." he began, but his voice trailed off.

"The mummy is really cool, isn't it?" Benny asked.

"It isn't *cool*," Dr. Snood snapped. "It is a valuable artifact from four thousand years ago. You must never touch it, or any of the things in this exhibit. Do you understand?"

The Aldens were stunned. Benny was only being friendly. Why was Dr. Snood getting so angry?

"Yes," Henry said. "We understand."

Dr. Snood's eyes moved quickly around the room, as if he were looking for something. Then, picking up his briefcase, he walked out without another word.

CHAPTER 3

Mysterious Footsteps

"I was just trying to be nice," Benny said, looking after Dr. Snood.

"I know," said Violet. "Don't feel bad."

"He's just a grumpy man," said Henry.

"But I wonder why," Jessie said. "Is it just that he doesn't like kids, or is something else bothering him?"

"Did you see how he was looking at the mummy when we came in?" Violet asked.

"And then he seemed so startled when he saw us," Henry added. "As if he'd been doing something wrong."

Before they could say any more, Pete came hurrying into the room. "Hi, kids!" he called out. "Sorry, I got stuck on a phone call. Have you been here long?"

"No," said Henry. "We just got here."

"And ran into Dr. Snood," Benny said.

"He didn't seem to be very happy to see us," Jessie explained. She couldn't help but wonder why Dr. Snood was being so mean to them when they were only trying to help the museum.

"Pete, what's an 'artifact'?" Benny asked, remembering one of the words Dr. Snood had used.

"An artifact is an object made by people a long time ago," Pete answered. "Like all these pieces here — the cups, pots, toys, instruments, and sculptures. We can learn a lot about people who lived a long time ago by studying the things they left behind."

"That makes all these objects very valuable," said Pete. "They're important — and they're also worth lots of money."

"Don't worry, we'll be careful," Benny assured him.

"I know you will," Pete said. "Now how about we get to work? We'll start by cleaning out the exhibit hall next door, where the exhibit will be set up for the public."

The Aldens followed Pete through a side door into a much larger room. It was filled with glass display cases and cardboard boxes. Everything was covered in dust, and the paint on the walls was chipped and peeling.

"Hey, isn't that a model of the solar system?" Henry asked, pointing to a group of balls in different sizes hanging from the ceiling.

"And there are some photographs of the moon over there," Violet added.

"The last exhibit in here was about outer space," Pete explained.

"And now it's just a mess!" Benny said.

"Well," said Jessie, rolling up her sleeves, "where do we start?"

In no time, the Aldens were busy. Pete went through everything in the room, dividing it into things to save and things to throw away.

While they were working, Dr. Dickerson arrived, a big, straw bag over her shoulder and a briefcase in her other hand. "Cleaning up the exhibit hall?" she asked.

"Yes, and the Aldens are helping," Pete said. "Since Tina is out and our cleaning crew can't do the extra work, the kids offered to help get the exhibit ready."

The Aldens waited to hear what Dr. Dickerson would say. They were afraid she might not want their help.

"That's great!" Dr. Dickerson said, a smile slowly spreading across her face.

"We're so glad you like the idea, Dr. Dickerson," said Jessie. "We'll do a great job, I promise."

"You can start by calling me Sam, like my friends do," she said. Then she turned to Pete. "How does Dr. Snood feel about the children helping out? I imagine he wouldn't like the idea." The corners of her

mouth were curled up in a small, mysterious smile.

"He doesn't seem to like kids at all," said Henry.

"You're right about that," said Sam.

"But how would you know that?" Pete asked. "You haven't met Dr. Snood yet, have you?"

"Oh — no, I haven't. But I'm sure I'll meet him soon," Dr. Dickerson said. She looked uncomfortable for a moment. "Anyway, I know how museum directors can be."

"Well, he agreed to it when I told him last night," Pete said. "I think it's because he knows we have no other choice."

As the children were leaving the museum that evening, they heard a voice behind them. "Hey, Aldens!"

They turned around and were surprised to see Lori Paulson walking quickly toward them, her orange bag swinging as she walked. She seemed just as surprised to see them.

"What are you doing back here again?" she asked.

There was an awkward silence as the children wondered what to say. They didn't want to be rude, but they knew the details of the exhibit were a secret.

"We're helping with the new exhibit, but Pete told us not to talk about it," said Henry at last, trying to sound firm.

His answer did not stop Lori from asking, "What's going to be in the exhibit? Did you see a mummy?"

"Actually, we haven't seen anything," Violet said, surprising everyone. She was very shy and didn't usually say much to people she didn't know well. "We've just been cleaning out the exhibit hall upstairs."

"So the exhibit will be upstairs?" Lori said. "And they must be preparing the pieces nearby. . . ." Now she seemed to be talking to herself, almost thinking aloud.

"We've got to get going," Henry said.

"All right!" Lori said. "Thanks!" She seemed to have learned what she wanted to know. She headed off in the opposite direction.

"I hope we didn't just give away something we shouldn't have," said Violet.

The next day, the children returned to the museum. Pete had other work to do, so he had told them to go right upstairs and get to work without him.

The Aldens came down the long, dark hallway. When they reached the exhibit hall, Jessie flipped on a light switch, filling the windowless room with light.

The Aldens carefully packed the last of the old outer space displays into boxes. They were so hard at work that the room remained eerily quiet.

Suddenly, Violet heard some footsteps in the hall. "That must be Sam or Pete," she said, expecting someone to appear in the doorway at any moment. But a few minutes passed, and there was nothing but silence.

"That's funny," said Violet.

"What?" asked Jessie.

"I just heard footsteps in the hallway," Violet said. She went to the door and looked down the long, dark hallway in both directions. There was nobody there.

"Maybe I was imagining it," Violet said.

The children went back to work, and a few minutes later, the sound of footsteps returned. "Hey — do you guys hear that?" Violet asked in a hushed voice.

Everyone listened, but the sounds in the hallway had stopped.

"What was it?" asked Jessie.

"I heard footsteps again," Violet said, going to the door once more. But when she looked out in the hall, there was no one there.

"I heard something, too," said Henry. He looked puzzled.

"What's the big deal?" asked Jessie. "Maybe there was someone in the hall, and whoever it was went into another room."

"But there aren't any other rooms in this part of the museum," Henry said. "Just this exhibit hall and the prep room. Why would someone be up here unless he or she was doing something with the Egypt exhibit?"

"Maybe it was Dr. Snood checking up on us," said Benny.

"Or Lori Paulson," suggested Henry. "She knows the exhibit's up here, and she seems awfully interested in it for some reason."

Suddenly, Benny's eyes grew wide. "Or maybe it was the mummy!"

"Oh, Benny," said Jessie.

"Well, it would sound quiet if it walked," Benny pointed out. "I mean, it's not wearing any shoes." He stood up, closed his eyes, stuck his arms out stiffly, and pretended to walk like the mummy.

The children's laughter was interrupted by Sam's arrival. She walked briskly into the room, carrying a large, straw bag.

"Oh, hello Dr. Dicker — I mean, Sam," Jessie said.

"Did you just get here?" Violet asked. "You weren't in the hallway a few minutes ago, were you?"

"No," said Sam. "Just got here."

"You didn't see anybody out in the hall, did you?" Henry asked.

"Nope," Sam said. "Why?"

"Oh, nothing," Henry said. "We just thought we heard someone a little while ago."

"Really?" Sam looked concerned. "There shouldn't be anybody up here besides us." Then she smiled. "Well, there's nobody there now," Sam said. "I'm glad to see you're getting the room ready. I've got a lot of work to do myself." Sam went into the prep room but came back out a moment later. "Have any of you been in the prep room this morning?" she asked. Her face was grim.

"No, why?" Jessie asked.

"Come see," Sam said.

The children went into the prep room, curious about what was the matter. As soon as they stepped in the door they could see why Sam was upset. The papers on Sam's desk were no longer in neat piles; instead they were moved around, and some had slipped onto the floor. The artifacts, which had been lined up in orderly rows, were now scattered about all over the tables.

The children's jaws dropped open.

"What happened?" asked Violet.

"I don't know," said Sam.

CHAPTER 4

The Mummy's Curse Strikes Again

Sam sighed heavily. "When I left last night, everything was neat and organized."

"You mean, someone came in and messed it up?" said Henry. "Who would do that?"

"And why?" added Benny.

Sam shook her head. "I just don't know."

"Maybe that's what those footsteps were," Violet said. "That might have been someone sneaking in here."

"But you said you didn't see anyone, right?" said Sam.

"No, when I looked out no one was there," Violet said.

Sam sighed again. "As if it isn't bad enough what happened to Tina, now this."

"It's the mummy's curse again!" said Benny in a hushed voice.

"Oh, Benny, Pete was just joking about that," Henry said.

"It will take me all day to get everything in order again," said Sam.

"I can help," Jessie suggested.

Sam smiled at her. "That would be great. And from now on, we all have to make sure this door is locked tight when we leave."

Henry, Violet, and Benny went back to the exhibit hall to continue packing up the outer space exhibit. Meanwhile, Sam and Jessie sorted through the papers on Sam's desk and put them back in the correct order. When they'd finished that, they started reorganizing the artifacts.

"These artifacts are very valuable and very fragile," said Sam. "So we must always be very careful when we touch them and always wear protective gloves."

Jessie nodded. She was good at being careful. They slowly began to go through the scattered artifacts. Sam picked up each piece and read off the number written on the bottom. Jessie searched through the printed cards to find the information that went with it.

When Pete arrived at lunchtime, Henry and Violet had just taken the last two boxes to the storage room. "Wow!" he said when he entered. "You've done a terrific job! Now we'll have to do something about those walls."

The Aldens looked around at the scuffed and peeling paint. It did look awful.

"Normally I'd hire a painting crew, but we don't have enough money," said Pete.

"Don't worry. We can handle it," Henry assured him.

"Great. Where's Jessie?" Pete asked.

"In here," Jessie called from the prep room.

Pete and the children joined Sam and Jessie. Sam told Pete about the mess she'd found that morning.

Pete looked as upset as Sam had been. "Who would have been going through your things?" he asked. "Make sure you keep these doors locked. Give Henry a key, too, so the kids can lock up when they go in and out." He headed out the door.

"Ready for lunch, Jessie?" Henry asked. "Pete said we could pick something out in the café."

"All right!" Benny said.

But Jessie wasn't paying attention. She was looking at the tables. She and Sam had gotten all the pieces organized again, but there was still something wrong. She couldn't figure out what it was.

"Jessie?" Henry said again.

"Oh, yes?" she said, startled out of her thoughts.

"Come on, let's go down to the café," Henry said.

As the Aldens left the prep room, Jessie took one last look at the objects on the table. Something just wasn't right.

When the Aldens returned from lunch, Pete called them into the prep room. "We have a surprise for you," he said.

The children walked inside and he motioned to the end of the room where Sam was standing. Where the giant crates had been, there was now a large, wooden box. It was completely covered with elaborate paintings of people and animals.

"What's that?" Benny asked.

"That's the mummy's case — its coffin," Sam explained, leading the children over to look. "We unpacked the crates."

"So that's what was in the other crate," Benny said.

"It's really beautiful," said Jessie.

"The Egyptians painted pictures of their gods on the mummy cases. They'd also paint things that the person liked when they were alive," Sam explained.

"Where's the mummy?" Benny asked.

"You can see for yourself," Sam said. She and Pete carefully lifted the heavy, wooden lid. They laid it on the table beside the coffin.

Everyone peered into the coffin. The mummy was lying inside with a large, painted mask over its face.

"Look at that!" Benny exclaimed.

"That's the death mask. It's molded from the person's face and made to look just like the person," said Sam.

The children stared down at the face in the coffin. Its wide eyes, outlined in black, stared up at them. There was black, straight hair painted on both sides. A gold and red headband painted with fancy designs crossed the brow.

"That's amazing," Jessie said. She couldn't take her eyes off the beautiful mask.

"Do you know how mummies were made?" Sam asked.

"They wrapped up the dead bodies in bandages?" asked Benny.

"That's part of it," Sam said. "Normally when a person dies, the body decays. But the ancient Egyptians came up with a way to preserve the body."

"And then did they wrap it?" Benny asked.

"Yes," said Sam. "They stuffed it with sand or sawdust to keep the body's shape. Then they wrapped it carefully in strips of linen cloth. They put jewels and magical charms in between the layers, to help the dead person reach the afterworld. It took *fifteen* days to bandage a mummy!"

"That's a long time," said Jessie.

Sam continued to explain. "Finally, they put the death mask over the mummy's head and placed the mummy in its coffin."

The children stood for a few more minutes looking into the coffin.

Then Sam said, "I wanted you to see the mummy with its mask on. Now I'm going to put the lid on and keep it closed until the exhibit opens."

Pete helped her lift the heavy, wooden lid off the table and replace it on top of the coffin.

As Jessie followed the others into the exhibit hall, she took one more look around the prep room. She still had the nagging feeling something was wrong. But what?

A few minutes later, the Aldens had begun work on the walls of the exhibit hall. Henry scraped and sanded the areas where the paint was chipped and peeling. Meanwhile, the other three laid drop cloths over the floor of the exhibit hall and the glass cases. When that was done, they began priming and painting. They worked all afternoon.

It was nearly dinnertime when Pete came up to see how they were doing. "It looks much better," he said.

The Aldens finished up the corner they'd been working on and stepped back to look.

"Yes, it does," said Jessie, "if I do say so myself."

She and the others closed up the paint cans and cleaned the brushes and pans before they left. As they were walking out, the Aldens talked about all the interesting things they'd seen and learned about ancient Egypt so far.

"That was cool to learn how they made a mummy," Henry said.

"And I like all those statues," said Violet. "Especially those two gold cats."

"And the baboon," Benny added.

"That's it!" Jessie cried.

"That's what?" asked Benny.

"I noticed something was wrong in the prep room this morning," said Jessie.

"We all did — someone messed everything up," said Henry.

"Besides that," Jessie said. "Even after Sam and I had gotten everything straightened out, I kept thinking something was wrong. But I couldn't figure out what it was. Now I remember — the baboon wasn't with the other statues."

"What do you mean?" Violet said. "Sam said that was everything for the exhibit."

"Well, I didn't see it," said Jessie.

"Maybe Sam just moved it somewhere else," suggested Henry.

"Or maybe whoever messed up the room stole the baboon," Jessie said. "Maybe that's why the room was all out of order — because the person was going through all the statues."

"Was there anything else missing?" Violet asked.

"I don't know," said Jessie. "That was the only thing I noticed."

"Why would someone steal that baboon?" Benny asked.

"Remember, Pete said the objects were all really valuable," Jessie said.

"That doesn't explain why they went through Sam's papers," Henry pointed out. "Those aren't valuable."

"But those papers have information about the artifacts," Jessie said. "Maybe they wanted to read about the artifacts, too." She thought for a moment. "And there's an information card to go with each piece. But I don't remember seeing one for the baboon. If we had, Sam and I would have noticed the statue was missing."

"So the person stole the statue and the card, too?" Violet asked.

"I guess so," said Jessie.

"We'd better tell Sam about this first thing tomorrow morning," said Henry.

"See?" Benny said. "That mummy's curse wasn't just a joke!"

CHAPTER 5

A Thief in the Museum

The Aldens arrived early at the museum the next morning. But this time, the door to the prep room was locked.

"That's good," said Henry. "Now no one can go in and make a mess or steal something."

While the children waited for Sam or Pete to arrive, they finished painting the last wall of the exhibit hall.

They were just cleaning their brushes when Sam appeared in the doorway.

"Hello!" she called, heading into the prep

room. The Aldens quickly put away all the painting supplies and followed Sam.

"Sam, we were wondering . . ." Jessie began. "Are these *all* the pieces for the Egypt exhibit?"

"Yes," Sam said, continuing to unload her bag.

"Are you sure everything's here?" Jessie asked.

Sam looked quickly at Jessie. "What do you mean?"

"Well, the first day we were here, Pete showed us some of the artifacts. And there was a little baboon . . ." Jessie said.

"Yes?" Sam said.

"Where's the baboon now?" Jessie asked.

Sam's eyebrows furrowed. "The baboon? It's . . ." She went over to the tables holding the artifacts and walked slowly from one table to the next. "How odd," she mumbled to herself. She walked around the tables again before walking quickly to the corner where the boxes were stacked. The Aldens watched as Sam picked up one box after another, making sure they were all empty.

At last, Sam turned around and looked back at the Aldens. "I don't know where it is," she said. She looked quickly around the room, but there was nowhere else that the baboon statue could have been.

"So you saw the baboon two days ago?" Sam asked.

"Yes," said Henry. "It was right on the table with the other pieces you'd unpacked."

"I remember because it was my favorite piece," said Benny sadly.

"When did you notice it was missing?" Sam asked.

"Yesterday," Jessie said. "And remember, someone had come in and messed everything up. . . ."

"Oh, my goodness," Sam said, sinking into her chair. "So we have a thief."

Everyone was silent for a moment.

Then Sam spoke. "We mustn't jump to conclusions. The statue may just have been misplaced."

"There may be other things missing, too," Jessie pointed out. "I just happened to notice that piece because it was Benny's favorite. Should I go through the list you have and see what else is missing?"

"No," Sam said. "You kids have done enough work already. Take a break for lunch."

"Shouldn't we tell Pete and Dr. Snood?" Henry asked.

"Yes, definitely," said Sam. "But not until we're really sure it's missing. I don't want to worry them if I don't have to."

When the Aldens came back from the café a short while later, they were pleased to see how bright and clean the exhibit hall looked with its fresh coat of paint.

"Now all we need to do is wash this filthy floor," said Jessie.

"And dust the display cases," Henry added.

Henry and Jessie each took a mop and a bucket from the supply closet and found a bottle of floor soap. Violet and Benny found rags and some glass cleaner.

They were returning to the exhibit hall

when Sam appeared in the doorway. "Jessie, I've decided I could use your help. I've got too many other things to take care of." She handed a set of papers to Jessie. "That's the printout of all the items we're supposed to have in the exhibit. You'll see I made a little *x* next to the baboon. Would you make sure there's nothing else missing?"

"Sure," said Jessie. She followed Sam into the prep room.

Sam sat back down at her desk. Jessie walked slowly around the tables, checking off each item on the list when she'd spotted it. She noted the cups and pots, the doll, the beautiful gold cat statues.

As she flipped through the list, Jessie noted happily that every item had a checkmark next to it except for the baboon, which had an *x*. She was pleased to see that no other items were missing.

Or were they?

Jessie looked back at the table. There had been a wooden flute, hadn't there?

She looked all around the tables, but there was no flute to be seen.

Then she looked at the paper she was holding. Had she somehow missed the listing for the flute? She quickly scanned down the list. The flute was not listed.

"Sam, this is really weird," she said.

"What is it?" Sam asked, looking up from her work. "Is there something missing?"

"No, everything on the list is here," Jessie said.

"Great," Sam said with relief.

"But I remember something that isn't here," Jessie said.

"What?" Sam asked, standing up.

"A wooden flute," Jessie said.

"Yes, of course," Sam said, going to look for herself. "I was planning to put that on display next to the harp. It isn't here?"

"No," Jessie said. "And what's even stranger, it's not on the list, either." She handed the list to Sam.

Sam flipped slowly through the list, looking carefully at each page. "You're right, the flute isn't listed." Then she looked at the tables. "And I don't see it anywhere." Sam made a note at the bottom of the list. "Another missing piece."

"Why isn't it on the list?" Jessie asked.

"I'm not sure," said Sam. "This is the list I got from the Egyptian Museum. Maybe they added the flute later and forgot to put it on the list." Sam smiled at Jessie. "Lucky for me you have such a good memory."

"Are you going to tell Pete about it?" Jessie asked.

"Yes, I'll go right now." Sam walked to the door. Then she turned around and looked back at Jessie. "Don't say anything about this to him, though. I don't think he'd want everyone to know that pieces of the exhibit were missing. You understand, don't you? Bad publicity for the museum."

"Yes, I understand," Jessie said.

After Sam had left, Jessie went into the exhibit hall. She told the others about the missing flute and that it had never even been on the list.

"I can't believe someone has been stealing things from the exhibit," Benny said.

"What's Sam going to do about it?" Henry asked.

"She went to talk to Pete, but she said we shouldn't say anything about it," Jessie said.

"Why not?" Benny asked.

"It would be bad publicity for the museum if people found out," Jessie explained. "Sam figured Pete wouldn't want everyone to know."

"That makes sense," Henry agreed.

"I can't believe there's a list of items that isn't even accurate," said Violet. "What good is that?"

"I have an idea," Jessie said. "Let's make our own list. Then we'll be sure of everything that's there — and we'll know if anything else disappears."

"Great idea," said Violet. "I'll help you."

"Benny and I will finish cleaning the display cases," said Henry.

Going to her backpack, which she'd left by Sam's desk, Jessie pulled out a small, blue notebook and a pen. She had written her name on the inside cover, but other than that, the notebook was blank. Jessie flipped open to the first page and wrote at the top: *Enter the Mummy's Tomb*. "You look at the table and tell me the items, and I'll write them down," Jessie said.

"Okay," said Violet. "Two gold cat statues . . ." she began. Slowly the girls worked their way around the tables, with Violet telling Jessie what was on each table, and Jessie writing the items in her notebook. She wrote down the name of the object and a short description so she'd remember what it was. It took a long time, but at last, they had an accurate list of everything that was there.

Sam returned as they were finishing the list.

"What did Pete say?" Jessie asked.

"He wasn't in his office," Sam said. "I'll have to catch him later." She looked at Jessie's notebook, which Jessie was just closing up.

"What are you doing?" she asked.

"Since that list wasn't accurate, Violet and I decided to make our own," Jessie said. She handed the notebook over for Sam to see.

"What smart kids you are," Sam said.

Just then they heard a deep voice in the next room. When they looked in, Pete was there talking with Henry and Benny.

"Hi, Pete," Violet said as she and Jessie joined the others.

"I was just telling the boys how great it looks in here." He walked around the room admiring the children's hard work. "Our regular cleaning and painting crews couldn't have done a better job."

The children smiled proudly.

"They've done a fine job, haven't they?" Sam said. "Pete, can I talk to you in here for a moment?"

"Sure," Pete said. "I'll see you tomorrow," he told the Aldens.

The kids knew that Sam was going to talk to Pete about the missing items. They wanted to stay and hear what he planned to do. But it was nearly dinnertime.

"See you tomorrow," Henry called over his shoulder.

CHAPTER 6

An Overheard Conversation

The next day, when the Aldens arrived at the museum, they found Sam carrying a large, framed picture into the exhibit hall.

"What's that?" Benny asked. The painting showed a group of Egyptian men and women. Their bodies were all turned sideways and looked stiff and angular. The edges of the painting under the glass were jagged and uneven.

"It's a painting on papyrus," she said. "That's what the Egyptians used since they didn't have paper. Isn't it amazing how the colors have lasted for thousands of years?"

"How beautiful!" Violet said. She loved to paint and always enjoyed looking at artwork.

"These paintings really make the exhibit complete," said Sam. "You see, the walls of the Egyptian tombs would have been covered with paintings depicting the dead person's life."

"Did you talk to Pete last night about the missing pieces?" Jessie asked.

"Yes," Sam said. "He's going to have new locks put on the doors and make sure the security guard comes by each night. We'll catch the thief." She smiled at Jessie's concerned face. "Don't worry so much."

"I just wish there was something I could do," Jessie began.

"There is," Sam said. "Help me hang these paintings."

The children spent the rest of the morning working with Sam.

First, Sam selected two maps to be mounted on the wall. One was a map of the world, showing the country of Egypt on the continent of Africa.

"Egypt is on the other side of the world from our country," said Violet.

"It's near the equator, so it must be hot there," Henry pointed out.

The other map showed the outline of ancient Egypt. "What's that big, blue line?" Benny asked.

"That's the Nile River," said Sam. "It was very important to the Egyptians. Egypt is a desert with very little rain. The people depended on the Nile for water to live and to grow their crops."

They hung the two maps right by the entrance to the exhibit.

Next, they put up an assortment of paintings that showed Egyptians in many different poses: eating, singing, dancing, and driving chariots.

Other paintings depicted Egyptian gods. They had human bodies and some had the heads of animals.

Some of the paintings had rows of tiny

little pictures. "What are those?" asked Benny.

"Those are hieroglyphics, a kind of Egyptian writing system," Sam said. "It was created over five thousand years ago. The pictures might stand for a sound, a letter, or a whole word."

Sam and the children stood in the center of the hall and looked around slowly.

"I'm going to get Pete to come up and see how great it looks," said Violet.

"I'll come with you," said Benny.

The two went downstairs to Pete's office. His door was closed and it looked dark inside. Violet knocked. As the children waited for an answer, they couldn't help overhearing the conversation in Dr. Snood's office next door, as his door was open.

"I'm worried because Ms. Delaney, the director of the Carson City Museum, called again. They're quite upset over there," Dr. Snood was saying.

"What did she say?" the children heard Pete ask.

"She said the Carson City Museum isn't happy about working with us on next year's festival. They feel we stole the Egypt exhibit away from them," said Dr. Snood.

Violet and Benny looked at each other, their eyes wide.

"That's crazy," Pete was saying.

"Well, that's how they feel," said Dr. Snood. "You know, for the past few years we've always worked well with them. That is, before you started here and suggested this exhibit."

"Maybe there's something we can do," Pete suggested.

"You work on it," said Dr. Snood. His voice sounded angry.

A moment later, Pete emerged from Dr. Snood's office. His face looked serious until he spotted the Aldens. "Violet, Benny," Pete said with a smile. "How's everything going?"

"We've put up all the paintings — want to come see?" Violet asked.

"I'd love to," said Pete. He turned back into Dr. Snood's office. "Reginald, would you like to come see how the Egyptian exhibit is going?"

"I've got to make a phone call," Dr. Snood said. "Then I'll come up for a quick look before my lunch meeting."

When they entered the exhibit hall a few minutes later, Pete broke into a huge grin. "This looks fantastic. I'm sure Dr. Snood will be pleased when he sees it."

Sam, who had been waiting with Jessie and Henry, said, "Oh, is he coming up?"

"Yes, he said he'd come up for a few minutes before his lunch meeting," Pete said.

Sam looked at her watch. "Is it lunchtime already? I've got to run."

"Can't you stay a few minutes to talk to Dr. Snood?" asked Pete.

"No, I'm meeting with the man who's designing the guide for the exhibit, and it may take all afternoon. I'll see you tomorrow." She went quickly into the prep room and grabbed her things. Then she was gone.

Dr. Snood appeared in the doorway a moment later. He walked slowly around the room, looking at the freshly painted walls, the clean glass cases, and the paintings the children had helped put up.

"I must admit, it does look nice in here," he said in a tight voice, as if it were hard for him to say something nice. "And where is Dr. Dickerson?"

"Sam had to leave in a hurry," Pete explained.

"You'd think our expensive Egyptian expert could make time to meet with me. We're certainly paying enough," he said. "Why are all the display cases empty?"

"We just cleaned them yesterday," Jessie said. "Sam is going to arrange the pieces soon."

"So I assume the artifacts are still in the prep room," Dr. Snood said, heading in that direction.

Pete turned to the kids. "I think he's pleased. You've done a great job. Why don't you take the afternoon off, and we'll see you back here tomorrow."

"Okay," Violet said. The Aldens went into the prep room to get their backpacks.

Dr. Snood was there, standing beside one of the tables of artifacts. He was holding one of the gold cat statues, turning it slowly around in his hands. He had a dreamy smile on his face, as if he were thinking of something far away.

As the Aldens watched, he put down the cat and picked up a bright blue sculpture of a hippo. He must have felt the children's eyes on him, because he suddenly looked up. The look on his face changed abruptly. Now he looked as if he'd been caught doing something he shouldn't be. He quickly put the hippo down.

"You kids haven't been touching these, have you?" asked Dr. Snood.

"No, we—" Henry began.

"Make sure you don't," said Dr. Snood in a stern voice. "And make sure the lid on that coffin stays closed."

"Of course—" said Jessie. Before she could say any more, he walked out.

The Aldens stood still for a moment, stunned by Dr. Snood's harsh behavior.

At last Jessie said, "I don't know which

was stranger: the way he was looking at those artifacts or the way he just spoke to us."

"I don't know, either," Henry agreed. "I wonder what he was thinking about when we first came in and he was holding the statues."

"It was as if he were in another world," said Violet.

"And then he got so angry all of a sudden," said Jessie. "And we would never touch the artifacts!"

"Maybe Sam told him about the thief and so he's worried the pieces aren't safe," said Henry.

"He doesn't seem to trust us much," Violet said.

"There was something else, too," Jessie said. "Did you notice how he called Sam 'our expensive Egyptian expert' in that nasty tone?"

"Sounds as if he's upset the museum is paying her so much money," Henry said.

"Or maybe he's jealous," Violet suggested. "Remember, Pete said Dr. Snood used to be a leading expert on Egypt? Maybe he doesn't like the fact that Sam may know more than he does now."

"You guys?" Benny spoke up at last. "Can we go? I want lunch!"

"Sure, Benny," Violet said.

She and Henry picked up their backpacks. But Jessie was still digging around in her backpack when the others were ready to go.

"What's the matter, Jessie?" Violet asked.

"It's nothing. . . . I just can't find . . ." She continued to dig in her backpack. At last she stood up, a puzzled look on her face. "It's not in there."

"What's not in there?" asked Violet.

"My notebook," said Jessie. "The one with the list of artifacts."

"Are you sure you put it in your backpack?" Henry asked.

"I think so," said Jessie.

"Have you looked at it since yesterday?" Violet asked.

"No," Jessie said, still puzzled. It wasn't like her to lose things.

"Maybe you left it around here some-where," Benny suggested.

The children spent the next few minutes searching the prep room — under the ta-bles, on Sam's desk, behind the coffin. Then they moved on to the exhibit hall and looked all over the room. The blue note-book was nowhere to be found.

"Maybe you left it at home," said Violet.

"I don't think so," said Jessie. "I didn't look at it there."

Benny frowned. "The mummy's curse strikes again!"

CHAPTER 7

The Feeling of Being Watched

The next morning, Pete met the Aldens at the door to the prep room. "Sam isn't here yet, but you can wait for her in there."

As Pete headed back down the hall toward the stairs, the children pushed open the door to the prep room. It was dark and quiet inside.

At the end of the room the Aldens could make out the coffin where the mummy lay.

For a moment no one said or did anything. The room felt creepy with no one around but the mummy.

Then Jessie broke the silence. "What are we waiting for? Let's go in." She led the way inside and turned on the light. Suddenly it was just an ordinary room.

"When do you think Sam will get here?" Benny asked.

"I wish she'd told us what she needed us to do today," said Jessie. "We could have gotten started — we have only two days left until the exhibit opens."

"I know what we can work on," Violet said. "Remember Sam said she was meeting with the person who's designing the guide for the exhibit? Well, what if we made a special guide for kids?" Violet asked.

"What do you mean?" asked Jessie.

"It could give some information about ancient Egypt that kids might like to know," Violet said.

"It could explain how they make mummies," Benny put in.

"And we could make up some games and activities about the exhibit, too," Violet added.

"This is like doing a report on Egypt, only more fun," Jessie said. "I'll go down to Pete's office and see if he has some books we can use for research."

"Great idea," Violet said. "I'll come with you."

When they had left, Benny said, "I'll make up some games for the guide. I'm good at games." He looked around the room for a place to sit. It was a small room. Most of it was filled with the tables of artifacts, waiting to be arranged in the display cases. Benny didn't think it would be right to sit down at Sam's desk. The little bit of extra space at the end of the room held the coffin. Benny remembered the mummy's curse and shivered.

"Why don't you go in the exhibit hall? You can sit down on the floor in there," Henry suggested, unlocking the door for his little brother. "I'm going to stay in here and look at the artifacts to get some ideas."

"Okay," Benny said. He pushed open the door to the exhibit hall. There were no windows and it was dark and eerily quiet inside. He felt on the wall for a light switch but didn't feel any. "Henry?" he called back into the prep room.

Henry was concentrating on the artifacts and didn't answer.

"Henry?" he called again.

"Yes?" Henry said at last.

"Where's the light switch?" Benny asked.

"It's over by the main entrance," Henry said.

"Oh, okay," said Benny. All he had to do was walk across the room and turn on the light. But for some reason he felt nervous. He felt as if he weren't alone in the room, as if someone were hiding in the darkness.

"This is silly," he said to himself. "That mummy has me spooked."

Benny began walking across the room. As he walked, he again had a strange feeling that someone was watching him. He could feel someone's eyes on him.

He stopped walking and looked slowly around. "Hello?" he said, his voice shaky in the large, dark, silent room. No one answered. "Hello?" he called again.

Benny felt a prickling sensation on the back of his neck. His palms began to sweat.

He walked quickly to the other door and was relieved when he found the light switch there. He turned it on and looked back around the room. Everything seemed so different in the bright light.

Benny sat down on the floor with his paper and thought for a moment. Then he began to draw a maze. It was supposed to look like a path through a tomb, and you had to find the mummy at the end.

But even with the light on, he didn't feel comfortable. He kept looking over his shoulder, sure that someone, not just a person in a painting, was watching him.

At last, Benny gave up and went back into the prep room to see what Henry was doing. He came in just as Violet and Jessie were returning from Pete's office, their arms full of books.

Henry was standing at one of the tables of artifacts, studying them. He looked upset.

"What's the matter?" Jessie asked.

Henry looked around at all the tables once more before answering.

"Remember that blue hippo that Dr. Snood was looking at?" he asked.

"Yes," Jessie said.

"I don't see it," said Henry.

The other three walked slowly around the tables. After a moment Jessie said, "You're right. It's not here."

"Not again," said Violet, putting down the books she'd been holding on Sam's desk. "That's the third piece missing!"

"Maybe Dr. Snood just put it somewhere else," Jessie said. "He looked very interested in it."

"Yes, maybe that's it," Violet agreed.

"We'll ask Sam when she comes in," Henry said. "We've got to find those pieces before the exhibit opens, and we've got only two days left." Then he noticed the books that Jessie and Violet had brought up. "It looks like you guys found a lot of books."

"We did," said Jessie. "Let's go in the exhibit hall and take a look."

The Aldens went into the next room

and sat down on the floor. They each took a book on their laps and began to flip through them. One book had beautiful photographs of pyramids and maps of Egypt. Another book contained pages of hieroglyphics. And Benny pulled out a book that told how to make a mummy. "Look at this." He pointed to a picture of a shriveled body that had been unwrapped from a mummy. "Gross!"

"But isn't it amazing that you're looking at the face of a person who lived thousands of years ago?" Henry asked.

"I guess so," said Benny, making a face.

Sam arrived a few minutes later. "Why all the grim faces?" she asked.

"Bad news," said Henry. "Another piece is missing. The little blue hippo."

The children all hoped that Sam would say something like, *Oh, that's okay. I just put it in a different room.* But instead, she said nothing. She looked at the children and then walked into the prep room. The Aldens followed as Sam went from table to table, a worried look on her face. Then she sank down into a chair and buried her head in her hands. Henry stood silently beside her, unsure what to do.

"This is terrible," Sam said at last, slowly lifting her head to look at Henry. "When did you notice it was gone?"

"Just this morning," said Henry. "I was looking for it because I remembered that Dr. Snood had been holding it yesterday when we left."

"Dr. Snood was holding it?" Sam said slowly.

"Yes," Henry said.

"That's . . . interesting," Sam said.

"You don't think he would have put it somewhere, do you?" Henry asked.

"I don't know," said Sam. "I hope that's the explanation. I'll have to ask him." She got up slowly and put her briefcase on her desk. "What have you been working on this morning?"

"We're doing a kids' guide for the exhibit," Violet said. The children excitedly told Sam all about it.

"That's a great idea!" Sam said. "I'll

take a look at it when you're done, and we can print copies downstairs." She unloaded some papers from her bag. When she had finished, she said, "I'm going down to speak to Dr. Snood. I'll see you later."

After she'd left, Violet turned to the others. "I hate to think that someone would steal things from the museum."

"I do, too," said Henry. "But what other explanation could there be for the missing pieces?"

"I wonder if it has something to do with the Carson City Museum," Benny said. He told the others what he and Violet had overheard the day before.

"You think someone at the Carson City Museum is so angry at the Greenfield Museum they would try to mess up the exhibit?" Jessie asked.

"Maybe, to make the Greenfield Museum look bad," said Benny.

"I think it's time we paid a visit to the Carson City Museum to see what we can find out," said Henry.

The children stacked the books in a corner of the prep room and gathered up their backpacks. After locking the doors behind them, they headed back home.

When the Aldens got home, they found Grandfather sitting in the living room, reading the paper and drinking a cup of coffee. "You're back early today," he said. "It's not even lunchtime."

"Grandfather, can we go to the Carson City Museum?" Henry asked.

Mr. Alden smiled. "You kids sure have caught the museum bug."

"Well . . ." Jessie looked at her sister and brothers. They hadn't mentioned anything about the missing pieces to their grandfather yet. But they never kept secrets from him. "There have been some strange things going on at the museum," she explained. "First it looked like someone had come into Sam's office and made a big mess. Then a few pieces from the exhibit disappeared."

"Really?" said Grandfather, looking concerned.

"Yes," said Henry. "No one seems to know what's going on."

"But you have an idea?" Mr. Alden asked. He knew the children were excellent mystery solvers.

"We don't know," Henry said. "But we found out that the director of the Carson City Museum was upset they didn't get the Egyptian exhibit. We're wondering if she could have anything to do with the strange things happening at the Greenfield Museum."

"Do you really think she would do something to hurt another museum?" Grandfather looked as if he couldn't really believe it.

"We don't know," said Jessie. "But we thought we'd just take a look around there and see what we can learn."

"You sure are good detectives," Grandfather said. "Whatever you find, I think you'll enjoy that museum. It has some nice exhibits."

Mr. Alden went to a cabinet in the front hall and pulled out a map. "Here are the bus routes to Carson City," he said as he unfolded the map and laid it on the dining room table. The children gathered around to look.

"You'll take the number-seven bus," Grandfather said, pointing to a purple line. "You see, it starts here in Greenfield and goes to Carson City. The bus will let you off at the museum." He traced the bus route with his finger.

"Sounds easy enough," said Henry.

Grandfather folded up the map and handed it to Jessie. He gave each of the children two tokens for the bus. "One for the way there, and one for the way home." The children tucked the tokens into their pockets. "You can get the bus right down at the corner. Call if you need me."

"All right," Jessie said as the children headed out the door. "We'll be home by dinnertime."

The children walked down to the corner, where a street sign and a bench marked the bus stop.

"Remember to stick together," Henry

said. "We don't want anyone to get lost."

The others nodded.

A few minutes later, a large, white bus pulled up to the stop. The children boarded the bus and put their tokens in the box. Then they found seats near the back of the bus.

The bus ride took about fifteen minutes. They were going down a busy street when Henry said, "I see the museum up ahead." He pulled a cord to signal the bus driver, and the bus came slowly to a stop at the next corner.

"Come on, you guys," Henry said, leading the way off the bus.

The children stood for a moment looking up at the museum before they went in. It was much larger than the Greenfield Museum, with white marble steps and columns in the front. There were three colorful banners hanging down between the columns, describing the exhibits on display. THINGS THAT SLITHER, read one banner with a large picture of a snake. Another banner said, CELEBRATIONS AROUND THE WORLD, and had a picture of a globe. The last said, GREAT PAINTERS OF OUR CENTURY.

"Well, here we are," said Jessie. "Let's go in and see what we can find out."

The children entered the lobby and paid the fee to enter. "Where should we go first?" Violet asked. They all looked around the lobby, which was much larger and more crowded than the one at the Greenfield Museum. None of them was really sure what they were looking for, or where they should look.

"I want to see that snake exhibit!" said Benny.

"Sounds like as good a place to start as any," said Henry.

The children went into the snake exhibit and walked around looking at interesting pictures of snakes and other reptiles. There were skeletons of giant boa constrictors and crocodiles, and diagrams of how their bodies work. Benny's favorites were the cases containing live snakes and lizards. A man who worked at the museum took out some iguanas and snakes for the children to touch and hold.

"That was great!" Benny said as the children headed into the exhibit next door, which was about holidays in different countries.

After that, the Aldens took a break for ice cream in the museum's café. It was similar to the one at the Greenfield Museum, but bigger.

"So far we haven't learned anything," said Jessie, disappointed.

"That's not true," said Benny. "We've learned a lot about snakes!"

"And how they celebrate New Year's in China," Violet added.

"That's true," said Jessie. "But we haven't learned anything to help us solve the mystery at the Greenfield Museum."

"That may be about to change," Henry said.

"What do you mean?" Violet asked, turning to look in the direction he was staring. Then she said, "I don't believe it!"

Jessie and Benny looked over to see Lori Paulson entering the cafeteria.

CHAPTER 8

A Museum Spy

As the children watched, Lori Paulson walked slowly down the cafeteria line. As usual, she had her bright orange bag slung over her shoulder. She selected a large cookie wrapped in plastic wrap and a cup of coffee. After she'd paid, she walked over to a table near the window. But as she went to sit down, her bag slipped off her shoulder and fell to the floor. A large pile of papers spilled out. Some slid beneath the table. "Oh, no!" she cried. "I'm so clumsy! I can't believe I just dropped all my stuff."

"I do that, too, sometimes," Violet said kindly, picking up some of the papers.

"I've had a really long day," Lori said.

"Really? Doing what?" Violet asked.

"Oh, I've just been here . . ." Lori said, and her voice trailed off.

"You've been here all day?" Violet asked. "You must really like going to museums."

"I do," Lori said. She smiled at Violet and then picked up the rest of her papers.

"What exhibits did you look at?" Violet asked.

"Oh, er . . . the dinosaurs," Lori said.

"Is there a dinosaur exhibit here, too?" asked Violet.

"Oh—no," Lori said. "I must have been thinking of the Greenfield Museum."

Violet said, "That dinosaur exhibit is great, isn't it?"

Then Lori sighed. "You know, actually I didn't see it. I only went to the Greenfield Museum because, well, there was something I was looking for. Something I had to get."

Violet was confused. "Oh," she said.

She wondered what Lori was talking about. Why did her story keep changing?

Violet reached under the table to get the last piece of paper. As she pulled it up, she saw it was a letter addressed to Lori with the words CARSON CITY MUSEUM at the top.

Lori glanced down at the letter Violet was holding. "Thank you for your help." She took the letter quickly, as if she was afraid Violet might try to read it. She stuffed it into her bag.

Just then a woman in a dark blue suit came into the cafeteria. "Ms. Paulson?" she said as she came over. "I'll be upstairs in my office in a minute if you want to talk."

"All right, Ms. Delaney. I'll be there," said Lori.

"Thanks for the help!" Lori said to Violet as she picked up her coffee and her cookie. "I've got to run."

Violet walked back to where her sister and brothers were.

"What was she doing here?" Henry asked, and then ate some of his ice cream.

"I don't know," said Violet, picking up

her spoon. "She seemed really nervous. She said she liked the dinosaur exhibit."

"Do they have one here, too?" Benny asked hopefully.

"That's what I asked," said Violet. "And she said she must have been thinking of the Greenfield Museum. But when I asked her how she liked that exhibit, she admitted she was really just at the Greenfield Museum because she was looking for something. Something she had to get," Violet said.

"I wonder what she meant by that," said Henry.

"Do you think she meant she had to get a sculpture of a baboon? Or a blue hippo? Or a flute?" Benny asked.

"Why would she steal those pieces?" Jessie asked.

"Maybe for the same reason most thieves steal things — for the money," said Henry. "Pete said they were very valuable. Or maybe she's a collector and she likes Egyptian art."

"Listen, you guys," said Violet. "It gets weirder. One of the things that fell out of her bag was a letter from the Carson City Museum."

"Why would someone here be writing to her?" Henry asked.

"I don't know," Violet said. "All I saw was that it was addressed to her. I wasn't going to read it. But before I could even give it back to her, she grabbed it, as if she didn't want me to see it."

"How odd," said Jessie.

"And then that woman came in and said that Lori should come upstairs to her office to talk," said Violet.

"Who was she?" asked Henry.

"I don't know," said Violet. "Her name was Ms. Delaney."

"We know she works for the museum if she has an office upstairs," Jessie pointed out.

"That name sounds familiar," said Benny.

"Let's go ask at the front desk," suggested Henry.

The children finished their ice cream and threw their garbage in the trash can. Then they headed out to the front desk.

"Excuse me?" Henry asked the man sitting there. "Is there a Ms. Delaney working here?"

"Ms. Delaney?" the man repeated. "Yes. She's the director of the museum."

"The director?" Henry said. "Oh, thank you."

As the Aldens walked away, Benny turned to the others, an excited look on his face. "That's why that name is familiar! She's the one Dr. Snood said had called him because she was angry about the Egypt exhibit!"

"Why do you think Lori is talking to her?" Jessie wondered.

"Do you think Lori's working for the Carson City Museum?" Henry asked.

"Doing what?" asked Violet.

"I'm not sure. Maybe trying to get information about the Egypt exhibit," Henry suggested.

Benny's eyes opened wide. "Like a spy?"

"Or maybe even more than that," Jessie said. "Maybe Ms. Delaney is so angry at the Greenfield Museum that she's hired Lori to ruin the exhibit."

"So you think Lori stole those pieces for

the Carson City Museum?" Violet asked.

"It could be," said Jessie.

Sam was working in the prep room when the Aldens arrived the next morning. When they asked her about the missing pieces, she said only that she didn't want to talk about them.

"She seems upset," Violet whispered to Jessie. The children spent the morning helping Sam arrange the artifacts in the glass cases. Only Henry and Jessie were allowed to carry the pieces. Benny and Violet brought the description cards to place beside them. Sam carried the most delicate pieces herself.

The children also worked on their guide. They studied the books Pete had lent them. Sam let them use her computer and printer. Jessie wrote an introduction to the exhibit. Henry typed up a brief description of ancient Egypt. Violet, who was an excellent artist, traced a map. She also copied some hieroglyphs out of a book and made a chart showing what each word meant. And she drew a beautiful picture of a mummy's death mask for the cover. Benny finished his maze and added a comic strip about mummy making.

When all the pieces of the guide were complete, they gave them to Sam. "Would you take a look at these, please?" Henry asked. "We want to make sure we didn't make any mistakes."

"I'd be happy to," Sam said, sitting down at her desk to read the children's work.

As Jessie stood next to Sam, she noticed a framed photograph on her desk. It showed four small cats lying on a bed. "Are those all your cats?" Jessie asked.

"Yes, those are my beauties," Sam said. "I have a weakness for cats."

A few minutes later, Sam had read through everything. "This looks great! You can make copies on the machine outside Pete's office," she suggested as she headed out to get some lunch. "Don't forget to lock the door when you go."

The children took all the pages and locked the door to the prep room behind them. As Sam had told them, they went downstairs to the copy machine by Pete's office. They made a stack of copies and stapled the pages together into little booklets. On top of each stack they put a copy of Violet's death mask cover.

The children were quite pleased with their work. They each picked up a pile of guides and headed toward the stairs.

But they stopped abruptly when they saw who was sitting a little way down the hall, outside Dr. Snood's office.

It was Lori Paulson.

"Not again!" Henry said.

Lori didn't notice them because she was studying a small, blue notebook she held in her lap.

"Hey!" Jessie cried. "That's my notebook!"

Lori looked up then. She stood up and started walking toward the Aldens. "Is this yours?" she asked, holding the notebook out in front of her.

"Yes," said Jessie. "It is."

"I saw your name on the inside cover," Lori said. "How convenient that you guys happened to be right here."

"Yes, how convenient," said Jessie suspiciously as Lori placed the notebook on top of the pile of guides she was holding. "Where did you find it?"

"It was right there on that bench," Lori said.

Jessie nodded slowly. She didn't remember carrying the notebook down here. How had it ended up there?

Benny groaned. His arms were getting tired from holding the stack of guides. "Can we get going before I drop these?"

"Sure," Jessie said. "See you later, Lori."

The Aldens walked back up to the exhibit hall and put the guides down on one of the glass cases. Sam was still gone.

"How did your notebook end up down on that bench?" Violet asked.

"That's just what I was wondering," said Jessie. "I don't remember bringing it down there."

"Maybe Lori didn't really find it there," Henry said.

"What do you mean?" Benny asked.

"Maybe she took the notebook," said Henry.

"I don't understand," said Benny. "Why would she take it?"

"She wanted to know all about the exhibit, right?" said Henry. "What better way to find out than by looking in Jessie's notebook, which listed everything?"

While he was talking, Jessie was slowly turning the pages of her notebook. The look on her face was growing more and more concerned.

"What is it, Jessie?" Violet asked.

"I think somebody's changed what I wrote!" said Jessie. She laid the book down on the display case where they could all see. She pointed to one of the items on the list. It had been crossed off so heavily it was hard to see what was written beneath. "See here? I don't remember crossing anything off." She flipped to another page. "And here, where it says 'gold cat statue'? I had written '*two* gold cat statues.' Someone crossed out the *two* and the *s* at the end."

"But why?" Henry wondered.

"I have a feeling I know," Jessie said. But before she explained, she started walking around the room, looking at the display cases. At last, she stopped in front of one of the cases. "There's one of the gold cat statues," she said. "But where's the other one?"

The children looked all around, but the other cat wasn't there.

"So you think Lori changed what was in here so you wouldn't remember there had been two cats?" Violet asked.

"Yes," said Jessie.

"Or maybe it wasn't Lori," said Henry. "Remember, Dr. Snood was holding that gold cat and he had that strange smile on his face? Maybe Lori wasn't lying about finding the notebook. Maybe it really was outside Dr. Snood's office. Maybe *he's* the one who stole the pieces and changed what was written in here."

"Why would he steal things from his own museum?" Benny asked.

"I don't know," said Henry. "But he's always acting so strange—holding the pieces as if they belonged to him, and yelling at us to make sure we don't touch them."

"He does collect Egyptian artifacts. Remember, they're all over his office," Jessie said. "Maybe he has even more at home— ones he's stolen."

"Or maybe he's the one trying to ruin the exhibit!" Henry said all of a sudden. "He's been against this exhibit from the start. Maybe he wants to prove he's right by making sure the exhibit fails."

"You know there's one person we haven't talked about," said Violet.

"Who's that?" Jessie asked.

"Sam," Violet said. "It would be really easy for her to steal these things."

"But why would she want to ruin her own exhibit?" asked Henry. "That would only make her look bad."

"That's true," said Violet.

A few minutes later, Pete came upstairs. "The exhibit looks great," he said, strolling from one display case to the next. "I can't believe we got it ready in time for tomorrow's opening!" He grinned at the Aldens. "Thanks to you guys."

"We enjoyed helping," Jessie said.

"Yes. We're having a little party tomorrow night," Pete explained. "We've invited the museum members and also the press. And of course you all must come."

"We'll be there!" Henry said.

"I have one more job for you to do," Pete said. "Would you call the local newspapers and remind them to come to the opening?"

"Why do you invite them?" Benny asked.

"They'll write articles about the exhibit in their newspapers," Pete explained. "When people read them, they'll want to come see for themselves. That's how we'll make sure we get lots of visitors for the exhibit."

"We'd be happy to call," said Henry.

"Great," Pete said. "The list of names and numbers is in my office. You can sit there and use my phone while I get some lunch."

"Okay," said Benny. "As long as you bring some back for us!"

CHAPTER 9

A Scary Surprise

The Aldens used Pete's office to make their phone calls.

Henry had already spoken to a man at the local television news station. Now he was calling the local radio station. "Hello, I'm calling from the Greenfield Museum," Henry said, just as Pete had told him to. "I wanted to remind you about the opening tomorrow night of our latest exhibit, 'Enter the Mummy's Tomb.'"

"We'll have someone there to cover it," said the man on the other end.

"Great," said Henry, hanging up the phone. Jessie checked the radio station off her list.

"Next is the *Greenfield Daily News*, the local paper," said Jessie. "The number is 555-6444."

Henry dialed and listened to the phone ring a few times. Then a woman answered.

"Hello, *Greenfield Daily News*," she said. "Can I help you?"

"Hello," Henry said. "I'm calling from the Greenfield Museum to remind you of our opening tomorrow night."

" 'Enter the Mummy's Tomb,' " said the woman. "Don't worry, we'll definitely send a reporter and a photographer."

"Yes, thank you," he said, sounding puzzled. He hung up the phone.

"What's the matter, Henry?" Benny asked.

"That was strange," he said.

"Why? What did they say at the newspaper office?" Violet asked.

"It wasn't what the woman said," Henry said slowly. "It was her voice. It sounded so familiar."

"Maybe it was some friend of Grandfather's," Benny suggested.

"Maybe," said Henry, puzzled.

"Anyway, we have a few more names to call," Jessie reminded him.

The children were finishing the phone calls when Dr. Snood came in.

"Where's Pete?" he asked.

"He's getting lunch," Jessie said. "He asked us to make some phone calls about the opening."

Dr. Snood turned and started to leave. He called over his shoulder, "Does Dr. Dickerson have everything ready?"

"Yes, she does," Henry said.

Dr. Snood stopped abruptly and turned around. He looked at Henry strangely. "*She?*" he repeated. "Sam Dickerson is a woman?"

"Haven't you met her?" Jessie asked.

Dr. Snood shook his head. "I've been so busy the past two weeks. Whenever I've gone up there, Dr. Dickerson hasn't been in. Pete scheduled a meeting for the three of us and . . ." He paused and then said awkwardly, "*she* couldn't come. Anyway, it doesn't matter. I saw the exhibit and it looks excellent." He walked slowly out of Pete's office.

"That's weird he never even met her," said Violet.

"Well, Sam did keep some pretty strange hours," Jessie pointed out as she placed the list on Pete's desk. "She'd come in late, leave all of a sudden, you know."

The Aldens left the office and went back upstairs. As they entered the prep room, Sam was there, talking on the phone. "Oh, you'll love this little cat," she was saying to the person on the other end. When she saw the children, she quickly stopped talking. "I'll speak to you later."

She hung up the phone.

"I was telling my friend about the new kitten I just got," Sam explained.

"*Another* one?" Jessie said.

"I couldn't resist," said Sam. She picked up her bag and put it over her shoulder. "Everything's ready for tomorrow. I'm heading home now."

"Hey, wait a minute," Benny said, noticing the coffin at the back of the room. "What about the mummy? Isn't that going to be part of the exhibit?"

"Of course," Sam said. "We'll move the coffin in tomorrow and open the lid. See you tomorrow at seven. Lock up when you go." She headed off down the hall.

The Aldens picked up their backpacks. "Well, tomorrow's the day," Jessie said, "and the exhibit's all ready."

"Looks like we beat the mummy's curse!" Henry said, giving Benny a playful punch on the shoulder.

Before he left, Benny took one last look around the prep room. At the back of the room was the brightly painted coffin. Benny walked over and gently placed his fingers on the edge of the lid, which was shut tight.

"Good night, mummy," Benny whispered. "Tomorrow's your big day."

The next day, the Aldens were at home eating lunch when Benny said, "I can't wait until tonight to see the opening of the exhibit."

"I just hope nothing else goes wrong," said Violet.

"Maybe we could just stop in and see if they need any last-minute help," Jessie said.

The Aldens biked over to the museum. When they arrived, they found Pete and Dr. Snood in the lobby. Pete was standing beside a pair of signs that read:

Enter the Mummy's Tomb
Upstairs Exhibit Hall
Opening at 7:00 This Evening
By Invitation Only

The signs were mounted on sturdy metal stands. With them was a pair of metal poles linked by a red velvet rope.

"Hello!" Pete said when he saw the children. Dr. Snood said nothing.

"Any last-minute jobs you need done?" Henry asked.

"None that I can think of," said Pete. He looked at Dr. Snood, who shook his head. "Sam isn't coming in until later, and we haven't even gone upstairs yet." Pete placed one of the signs in the center of the lobby, next to the main desk. He stood back to see how it looked.

Then he turned to the Aldens. "Actually, there is something. Can you put these up in front of the entrance upstairs so no one will go in until tonight?" He motioned to the sign and velvet rope.

"We'd be happy to," Henry said, picking up the sign.

Jessie and Violet each took one of the metal poles. They walked slowly upstairs.

As they came down the hall, they could see that both the prep room and the exhibit hall were dark and deserted.

But when they reached the prep room, they stopped short.

Something was wrong.

The door of the prep room was open. The children had locked the door before they'd left the night before. Who would have opened it? Pete had said Sam wasn't in yet, and he and Dr. Snood hadn't been upstairs that morning. The only other person who would have a key was the security guard, and she had no reason to go in there.

Had someone broken into the prep room?

The children looked at each other silently. "What's going on?" Henry said quietly.

Jessie shrugged her shoulders.

"Hello?" Henry called, slowly pushing the door open farther. The door creaked as it slowly swung open.

The Aldens peered into the dark room. Everything looked just as they had left it the evening before. Sam's papers were stacked neatly on her desk. Her chair was pushed in underneath. The coffin was still at the back of the room.

Jessie bent down and studied the lock on the door.

At last Violet asked what they were all wondering. "Did someone break in?"

"Looks that way," Henry said. "We locked the door last night, so whoever it was must have picked the lock."

"Wait a minute," Jessie said suddenly. "If someone was trying to get in, they'd pick

the lock from the *outside*, right?" she asked.

"They'd have to," said Henry.

"Well, look at these scratch marks." The children bent and looked where Jessie was pointing.

"So?" Benny asked.

"If someone was trying to get in, he or she would be on the outside of the door, right?" Jessie asked. "But the scratches are on the *inside*."

"So this lock was picked from the inside," Henry said.

"So that means . . ." Violet began.

"Someone was trying to break *out*," said Jessie.

The children looked back into the room. They looked all the way down to the other end where the coffin lay. And then they noticed something they hadn't noticed before.

Something even more frightening than the picked lock.

The lid of the coffin was open.

CHAPTER 10

The Truth Comes Out

"It was the mummy!" Benny cried. "It escaped!"

The lid of the coffin wasn't completely open, but it was pushed back several inches. It definitely was not the way it had been left the night before.

From across the room, it was too dark to see if the mummy was still inside.

"That's ridiculous, Benny," said Jessie. But she didn't sound sure.

"Then who was it?" asked Benny.

"I don't know," said Jessie. "But it wasn't

the mummy. The mummy has been dead for thousands of years."

"Come on, let's go take a closer look," Henry said.

The children began walking slowly to the other end of the dark room. They didn't take their eyes off the coffin. Benny lagged behind, afraid of what they might find — or not find — when they got there.

The coffin was exactly where it had always been, its painted designs visible even in the dim light. When they'd crossed the room, the children stood a few feet away, just looking at it.

They knew the mummy couldn't get up and move. They knew, as Jessie said, that it had been dead for thousands of years. But in the darkness, with the lid of the coffin slightly open, somehow anything seemed possible.

Henry took a few steps closer.

He was trying to peer inside the gap left where the lid had been pushed back. But the light was so dim that it was hard to see.

"Is the mummy still there?" Benny asked nervously.

"Yes, I think so," Henry said, squinting and moving closer.

"This is silly," Jessie said at last. She walked quickly back to the door and switched on the light.

Henry stepped up to the coffin and looked in. He could see the magnificent death mask peering up at him from inside the coffin. "Yes, there it is," he said, breaking into a smile.

The others breathed a sigh of relief and moved closer to see for themselves.

"There's something else in there, too!" Benny cried, pointing in the coffin.

The other children peered in. There was a large, straw bag tucked in next to the mummy.

"That's Sam's bag," Violet said. "What's it doing in there?"

Benny looked inside. All he saw inside was a brown-paper bundle. He put it up on the table. Before Henry could stop him, Benny had begun unwrapping it.

"I don't think you should —" Henry began. But he stopped speaking when he saw what was in the package. "I don't believe it!" he said.

"It's the missing gold cat," Benny said.

The children looked at each other, speechless.

"I'll go get Pete," Jessie said, walking toward the door.

A few moments later, Jessie returned with Pete — and Dr. Snood.

Jessie showed them the lock on the door. "See, here are the scratches."

The two men studied it. "This was definitely picked from the inside," Dr. Snood agreed. "Just as you said."

Then they walked to the back of the room and looked at the open coffin. "You children didn't open this?" Dr. Snood asked.

The children all shook their heads.

"Help me," Dr. Snood said to Pete. Together they lifted the lid off and placed it gently on the table. Then they both walked slowly around the coffin, examining the mummy and the death mask.

"I don't know why someone opened the coffin, but fortunately the mummy doesn't appear to be damaged," Dr. Snood said at last. He sounded relieved.

"There's something else," Henry said.

Dr. Snood looked up from the mummy. "What is it?"

Henry motioned to the gold cat. "We just found this — in Sam's bag," said Henry.

Dr. Snood picked up the statue. "In her bag, you say?" He strode over to Sam's desk. "I don't know what's going on, but I think it's time I had a word with Dr. Dickerson." He picked up the telephone.

"No," Jessie said.

Dr. Snood spun around in surprise.

"I mean, please let me call," said Jessie quickly. "I have a plan."

Dr. Snood looked at her for a moment and then nodded. "All right," he said.

Jessie picked up the phone and dialed Sam's number. She looked nervous. "Hello, Sam," she said after a moment. "It's Jessie, at the museum. Pete asked me to give you a call. He needs to see you."

She listened for a moment before she spoke again. "I don't know, he didn't say. He just asked that you come right away."

Again she listened, then said, "No, Dr. Snood is out at a meeting."

At last Jessie smiled. "All right, we'll see you soon."

She hung up the phone.

"Why did you tell her that — about Pete asking you to call and Dr. Snood being out?" Henry asked.

"I know it isn't right to lie," Jessie said. "But I didn't think Sam would come if she knew *Dr. Snood* wanted to see her. I've noticed that she's always avoiding him."

"That does seem to be true," Dr. Snood agreed.

"I guess you might say I've . . . set a trap," Jessie said.

"Very smart, young lady," Dr. Snood admitted.

Jessie smiled and felt her cheeks turning pink.

Pete grinned. "I told you these kids were good."

"I have a question," said Henry. "Has Sam told either of you about the pieces missing from the exhibit?"

"What?" the two men said. They looked at each other and then back at the children.

"Pieces *missing*?" asked Pete. "I've heard nothing of the kind."

"Neither have I," said Dr. Snood.

"We noticed some pieces missing, like a small baboon sculpture, and the little blue hippo, and a flute, and this gold cat. Sam said she had told you," said Jessie.

"No one said anything to me," Dr. Snood said. He seemed to be straining to remain calm. "When Dr. Dickerson comes, we'll get to the bottom of this. Pete and I will wait in here until she comes," Dr. Snood said, stepping into the exhibit hall.

When the two men had gone, Violet said sadly, "I hate to think that she's the one who's been stealing the pieces all along. She's so nice."

"I agree," said Jessie. "But she could still be a thief."

The Aldens waited for Sam to come. No

one felt much like talking. The only sound was the clock ticking on the wall.

Finally, the children heard footsteps in the hallway. "That must be her now," Jessie whispered.

The footsteps came closer, and then Sam stood in the doorway. "What's the matter?" she asked.

Then she spotted the statue on the table. "What's this doing in here? I put this —" She stopped abruptly as Dr. Snood stepped into the room, with Pete behind him.

For a moment, Sam and Dr. Snood just looked at each other.

Then a slow smile spread across Dr. Snood's face. It was not a happy smile. Instead, he looked very, very angry.

Sam sighed heavily and looked at the ground.

"So it's you," Dr. Snood said, his voice tight. "Even under all that red hair, I'd recognize you anywhere. I hoped I'd never see you again."

"Hello, Reggie," Sam said.

"What's going on?" asked Benny.

Dr. Snood turned to the children. "We've found our thief," he said. "Her name is Samantha Peters."

"It was," said Sam. "I've married. Now I'm Samantha Dickerson."

"You two know each other?" Pete asked.

"Yes," said Dr. Snood. "Dr. Peters — or Dr. Dickerson, if you prefer — was my partner many years ago, before I became the director here. We were digging in an Egyptian tomb. She was a brilliant Egyptologist, and everything was going well. Until I realized I could never work with her again."

"Why?" asked Benny.

"Shall I tell them?" Dr. Snood asked Sam.

She looked away, refusing to answer.

Dr. Snood turned back to the children. "She suggested we might take a few 'souvenirs' from the dig — small statues to keep for ourselves or sell. I told her, definitely not. But it sounds as if that's exactly what she's been doing here."

"Is it?" Violet asked Sam in a soft voice.

Sam was looking at the floor. She sighed again. At last she looked up at the faces of the children. Her face looked sad and tired. "Yes, I have," she admitted at last. "When Pete asked me to run this exhibit, I was very happy. I haven't been making much money lately. I thought I'd be able to pocket a few pieces and make some quick cash. I was planning to sell them to a rich collector I know."

"That's who you were talking to on the phone about a cat, wasn't it?" asked Jessie.

"Yes," Sam said. "When I found out that Dr. Snood was the director here, I was afraid he'd catch me. So I had my hair curled and dyed red. I went by my married name and called myself Sam so people would assume I was a man. Unless they met me, of course."

"So that's why you've been avoiding Dr. Snood," Jessie said.

"Yes," said Sam. "When Tina got hurt, I was pleased that Pete suggested you children would help me. I figured I could slip anything past a bunch of kids." She raised her eyebrows. "But I didn't realize who I was dealing with. You Aldens are smart. And you don't give up."

"No," Henry said. "We don't. Not until we've solved the mystery."

"So you never told anyone that those pieces were missing, did you?" asked Violet.

"Of course not," said Sam. "I didn't think you'd even notice if a piece was gone here and there. That's why I didn't take them all at once. I hadn't counted on you having such good memories. I had to pretend I was surprised each time you noticed another one missing. But I figured that if you kids were the only ones who knew, then I was safe."

"But then why did you give me that list to make sure nothing was missing?" asked Jessie.

"I made up that list myself. I left off the pieces I'd already taken," Sam said.

"What about my notebook?" Jessie asked. "Did you take it?"

"I did," Sam said. "You let me look at it,

and I never gave it back. I changed it, too. I tried to make it look like your handwriting, so you wouldn't realize. Then I left it by Dr. Snood's office, so you'd think he'd taken it, not me."

"What about the lock on the door and the open coffin?" asked Henry. "Did you do that?"

Sam nodded. "That's where I was hiding the pieces," she said.

"In the coffin?" Benny asked, shocked.

"I knew no one would look in there," she said. "Last night I came back here very late, after everyone had left. I was planning to take out the last of the pieces. But then the security guard came by, just as I was about to leave. I quickly turned off the lights so she wouldn't see me. But then she did something I hadn't expected." Sam laughed a short laugh. "She thought no one was in here, so she locked the door. I was locked in."

"And you had to break out," Henry said.

"Exactly," said Sam. "Good thing I know how to pick a lock. But in my hurry I left the coffin open and forgot to lock the door behind me. And I accidentally left the most valuable piece here — that gold cat."

While they were talking, Pete had quietly gone over to the telephone and made a phone call. A police officer appeared in the doorway just as Sam was finishing her story.

As the police officer led her away, Pete said, "It looks as if the mummy's curse is on Sam."

James Alden and his grandchildren arrived at the museum that night just before seven o'clock.

"I can't wait to see how everyone likes the exhibit," Benny said.

"And I can't wait to see what you've all been working on," Grandfather said.

"Hello, Aldens," Pete said, coming over as soon as he saw them. He brought Dr. Snood with him. The Aldens were surprised to see how happy Dr. Snood looked.

"James, good to see you," Pete said. He introduced Dr. Snood to James Alden.

"The exhibit looks great," said Grandfather.

"We couldn't have done it without your grandchildren," Pete said.

"I must admit I had my doubts at first," Dr. Snood said. "But I was wrong. They did a great job with the exhibit — and they caught a criminal!"

"That is their specialty," Grandfather said proudly.

"Can I tell you something, Dr. Snood?" Jessie asked in a quiet voice.

"Yes," Dr. Snood said.

"We thought *you* might be the thief," she said.

"*Me?*" he said. And then he did something they had never seen him do. He began to laugh. "Why me?"

"Well, we kept seeing you looking at the pieces, and then they'd be missing," said Jessie. "And there always seemed to be something bothering you."

Dr. Snood was silent for a moment. Then he spoke. "You children are wise beyond your years. There has been something bothering me, and it took this exhibit for me to realize it."

"Realize what?" Pete asked.

"I realized, as I watched this exhibit being put together, how much I miss Egyptology. That's my real love. So I'm stepping down as director. I'm going to lead a dig in Egypt next year."

"Excuse me," said a voice behind the children.

They turned around and were surprised to see Lori Paulson.

"Hello, Ms. Paulson," Pete said.

"What are you doing here?" Benny couldn't help asking.

Suddenly Henry laughed. "I think I know," he said. "You're a reporter for the *Greenfield Daily News*, aren't you?"

"How did you know?" Lori asked, surprised.

"When I called the newspaper yesterday, you were the one who answered, weren't you?" Henry said.

Lori nodded.

"I knew your voice was familiar," Henry

explained. "I just didn't figure out it was you until now."

"I've just started working there," Lori explained. "I'm an assistant in the Arts and Entertainment section. I was trying to make a name for myself by bringing in a report on the new exhibit. The museum was keeping it all such a secret. I thought there had to be something important going on. I wanted to get the story before any other reporter."

"So that's why you were always at the museum asking questions," said Benny.

"I was hoping you kids would tell me something," said Lori. "I listened when you were in the café and made notes in my notebook."

"So that's what you were hiding under the table that day," Henry said.

"I also sneaked up to the exhibit hall a couple of times and tried to peek in," Lori told them.

"We heard your footsteps," Violet said.

"And I did something I regret." Lori looked down at her feet and then back at the children. "One day, I sneaked into the prep room and went through the papers on the desk and looked at the artifacts. I was hoping to learn something to put in the article. But I heard a sound and rushed out before I had a chance to put things back. I'm afraid I left quite a mess."

"What were you doing at the Carson City Museum?" Henry asked.

"I heard they'd tried to get this exhibit, too," said Lori. "So I called them to find out. They wrote to me, and then finally gave me an appointment with the director the day I saw you there."

"And what did she have to say?" Dr. Snood asked.

"She told me at first they were disappointed they hadn't gotten the exhibit," Lori said. "But when she talked with Pete Miller, they came up with some ways the two museums could work together in the future."

"Good work," Dr. Snood told Pete.

"Why were you being so secretive?" Jessie asked Lori.

"I was afraid that if you knew I was a reporter you wouldn't tell me anything," Lori said.

"We thought you were a spy," said Benny.

"A spy?" Lori said. And they all burst out laughing.

"As it turns out," Pete said, "there is quite a story behind this exhibit. And I think the Aldens are just the ones to tell it."

The children spent the rest of the night telling Lori everything that had gone on at the Greenfield Museum while the exhibit was being prepared.

The next morning, Jessie picked up the newspaper at the front door. She brought it in to the kitchen, where the whole family was sitting, eating Mrs. McGregor's special blueberry pancakes for breakfast. Jessie turned straight to the Arts and Entertainment section. There, on the front page, was a picture of the four Aldens standing next to the mummy, and an article written by Lori Paulson, staff reporter. The headline read, ALDEN CHILDREN KEEP MUMMY'S CURSE FROM COMING TRUE.

THE MYSTERY AT
SKELETON POINT

created by
GERTRUDE CHANDLER WARNER

Illustrated by Hodges Soileau

The Mystery at Skeleton Point
created by Gertrude Chandler Warner;
illustrated by Charles Tang.

ISBN 978-0-8075-5520-0

Contents

CHAPTER 1

Not-So-Funnybones

The Alden family loved nothing better than long family car trips. They enjoyed playing games, telling stories and jokes, and having roadside picnics. Even in the car, they kept themselves busy with jobs.

Grandfather Alden's main job was driving, of course, plus laughing at his grandchildren's jokes and listening to their plans.

Since twelve-year-old Jessie was the best map reader, her job was to give Grandfather directions.

Benny liked to help Grandfather with directions, too. Now that he was six, Benny could read. His job was to call out the road signs.

"Shady Lake, six miles!" he announced when they passed a sign on their way to visit Grandfather's cousin Charlotte. "How far is that?"

"Way too far," fourteen-year-old Henry joked. He had squeezed himself between Benny and their ten-year-old sister, Violet so the two younger children could have the window seats. Henry's job was to not get twisted into a pretzel while Benny read road signs and Violet wrote in her diary.

"Don't forget to write a page about the scary house," Benny reminded his sister.

Now that the family was almost there, Jessie folded up the map and put it away. She unfolded a news clipping and a letter Grandfather's cousin had sent the week before. "Cousin Charlotte says to watch for a fork in the road right after the general store. There's a dirt road that goes to Skeleton Point if we want to stop. The other road goes to town."

"Read the spooky part again," Benny begged Jessie. "About the skeleton and the statues with no hands near the house at Skeleton Point."

"I can't, Benny. I have to watch the road," Jessie said. "Besides, the article she sent is mainly about her buying Skeleton Point, and some silly things people said about the skeletons that are in the house."

Grandfather drove slowly, looking for the turnoff. "Back when Charlotte and I were young, a real family lived there, not just skeletons for the medical school," Grandfather said. "The two of us often rowed across the lake to Skeleton Point. We never did get a good look at the property itself, but now that Charlotte owns it, we will!"

"Why is it called Skeleton Point?" Benny asked.

Grandfather smiled in the rearview mirror. "Some local people used to say there was a burial vault on the property. But it turns out the whole family is buried in the town cemetery. I don't think there's any such thing."

"What about the Walking Skeleton?" Benny asked. "Did you ever see that?"

Grandfather chuckled again. "Oh, that tale is something new — probably just someone pulling a prank. Charlotte said the story has to do with Dr. Tibbs's skeleton collection. He was the last owner before Charlotte bought the place. He collected skeletons for the medical school. I gather he sometimes put them in the windows to scare off trespassers."

A few minutes later, Benny forgot all about skeletons when he spotted his favorite kind of road sign: ICE CREAM AHEAD. "Can we stop? Lunch was a long time ago."

Everyone in the car laughed. For Benny, lunch always seemed like a long time ago.

Grandfather pulled up in front of the Shady Lake General Store. The Aldens got out to stretch their legs.

Violet sniffed the fresh air. "I like that woodsy pine smell. Now I know we're really on vacation."

"I like stopping for ice cream," Benny

said. "That's how *I* know we're really on vacation."

The children entered the old store. They made their way past fishing poles, garden rakes, and camping goods. When they came to a freezer full of homemade ice cream, they lined up behind the other customers who were also waiting for cones.

Nearby, several older men and women sat in a booth. They were playing cards and eating ice cream with long spoons.

While he waited, Benny tried not to stare.

"Well, young fellow, I hope you're not trying to see what cards I'm holding," one of the cardplayers said with a twinkle in his eye. "Your eyes are bigger than my ice-cream bowl."

Benny felt his ears get red. "Are you playing Go Fish?" he asked. "That's what we played in the car when we drove from Greenfield. Only now it's time for Go Eat Ice Cream, not Go Fish."

Everyone at the table chuckled.

"I'm getting chocolate ice cream," Benny continued. "And know what? We're going to Skeleton Point. Grandfather's cousin Charlotte bought it — even the skeletons. She asked us to help her fix up the house. We might even get to stay there overnight."

The players looked up from their cards when they heard this.

"Well," one silver-haired lady said, "you must be very brave. A lot of strange things have been going on at Skeleton Point ever since Charlotte bought Dr. Tibbs's old place."

Another man at the table put his finger to his lips. "Now, don't go scaring the boy with all that foolish talk about the Walking Skeleton."

The woman ignored the man. "Well, don't say we didn't warn you. I heard from William Mason, who's working out there, that there's a skeleton in the house trying to turn into a real person again. If you ask me, that's why some of those statues have missing parts."

Now Benny's eyes were bigger than dinner plates.

"Pay no attention," another cardplayer told Benny. "Everything's been falling down at Skeleton Point for years, especially those statues. I was glad to hear Charlotte's going to fix up the place. That'll stop all this Walking Skeleton nonsense."

"Maybe the Walking Skeleton is a real person already," Benny said. "I'm a walking skeleton, too. Only I have muscles on top of my skeleton."

The cardplayers laughed again and returned to their game.

When the Aldens got their cones, they sat on the front porch of the general store to enjoy their ice cream.

"Where to next?" Grandfather asked when everyone had finished. "As if I didn't know."

"Skeleton Point!" the children cried at the same time.

"Skeleton Point it is," Grandfather said.

Soon he slowed down when he came to a hand-painted sign nailed to a tree. A picture of a skull and words painted in dripping red paint warned, SKELETON POINT — KEEP OUT.

"Does that mean us?" Henry asked.

"Not at all," Grandfather said. "Charlotte said if we want to take a look at her property, we can go anytime. She keeps the driveway closed off to discourage trespassers. I'll park down here while you children run up and take a quick look around."

Violet zipped up her jacket. "See you in a little bit, Grandfather."

"It's so quiet," Benny said in a hushed voice as they walked through the dark, misty woods.

The next moments were not quiet at all, as a burst of barking broke the silence.

Startled, Benny grabbed his sister's arm.

"It's okay," Jessie said. "It's a dog."

A chocolate-brown Labrador retriever, bounded toward the children, gave one last bark, then ran off.

"I'm glad that was just a dog, not the Walking Skeleton!" Benny said as they approached the house.

"Whoa, maybe *that* is!" Henry pointed to a bony figure moving toward the mansion. As they watched, the figure vanished.

The children froze. Jessie and Henry tiptoed toward the house.

"Whoever — or whatever — that was is gone," Jessie said when she came back for Benny and Violet. "There's nobody around. Come see the house. It's a little spooky, but beautiful, too."

Indeed it was. The children passed an empty reflecting pool full of leaves. On each side stood several moss-covered statues — goddesses, cherubs, angels, even a stone lion. The figures were cracked, and a couple of them were missing arms or hands.

"It's so sad that they're all crumbling and ruined," Violet said when she came closer.

Close up, the stone house wasn't as big as it looked from a distance. Its long windows and tall doors made it seem larger than it really was.

"The house will be so pretty after it's fixed up," Violet said as they walked along the stone porch.

Henry saw something dark hanging off the stone railing. He held up a long black T-shirt painted with a skull on the front and skeleton bones on the back. "What's this doing here?"

"What are *you* doing here?" a strange voice said from somewhere nearby.

The children heard thrashing again, then a splash in the distance. But no one appeared, and the voice did not speak again.

Henry hung the T-shirt on the railing. "We'll have to tell Charlotte there's a trespasser on her property. And that one didn't sound like a dog."

Jessie jiggled the doorknobs of several doors, but none of them opened. "I wonder if anyone is inside." She stopped in front of one of the tall windows. When she tried to speak, no words came out.

"What's the matter?" Henry took a few more steps and looked inside. There, peering out of the window, was a skeleton! It stood on bony legs and grinned out at the children. "The Walking Skeleton?" Henry said, in a dry whisper. It took him and Jessie a moment to realize that the old skeleton was harmless. "Hmm. Well, it's certainly not walking anywhere," Henry said, noticing the wire that held it up.

Finally, Jessie found her voice again. "It must be one of those medical skeletons Grandfather told us about," she whispered, so the younger children wouldn't hear. "Let's show it to Benny and Violet right away so they don't get a sudden surprise."

"Good idea," Henry agreed. "Hey, guys, come over here if you want to see what a complete skeleton looks like. It's one of the ones Dr. Tibbs must have used to teach students at the medical school."

Benny and Violet walked over to the window.

"Oooh." They stared at the skeleton staring back at them.

"Oooh," an owl — or something that sounded like an owl — echoed in the distance.

Jessie went down the back steps. "Let's see if this path leads to the lake."

The children walked along until the

path ended on a point overlooking the lake. From there, a set of wooden steps led to a small, sandy beach below. A yellow rowboat bobbed on a dock.

A loud splash broke through the silence.

"Aaah!" the Aldens cried.

Something much larger than any duck — and much hairier — broke the surface of the still, foggy lake.

Benny took Jessie's hand. "What was that?"

The hairy creature disappeared under the water again just as more fog rolled in.

"Maybe the Walking Skeleton turned into a swimming skeleton," Benny said.

Jessie squeezed Benny's hand. "Don't worry, it's just a swimmer." But she wasn't so sure.

The children took one last look at the mist-covered lake, then hurried back to Grandfather and his warm, cozy car.

CHAPTER 2

The Walking Skeleton

"Goodness," Grandfather said when his grandchildren returned from Skeleton Point. "You look as if you've seen a ghost."

"Not a ghost, Grandfather — a monster in Shady Lake!"

"Goodness, that must have been quite a fright," Grandfather said. "What about the Walking Skeleton?"

"We found a skull T-shirt hanging off the porch," Henry answered. "And one of Dr. Tibbs's skeletons was hanging in a window, too."

"You'll have to tell Charlotte all about your sightings." Grandfather turned onto the main road and headed to the town of Shady Lake. "She'll want to hear everything. Here we are."

Grandfather pulled into the driveway of a snug blue house set behind a garden full of flowers. Cousin Charlotte, who was tall and white-haired like Grandfather, stood in the garden talking with an older man.

When she saw the Aldens' car pull in, Charlotte quickly came over to the car.

"Oh, James — and your wonderful grandchildren! I'm so happy you're here at last," Cousin Charlotte cried. "I've been gardening out front so that I would spot you right away. Come meet my visitor." She turned to the man she had been speaking to. "James, this is William Mason. William, this is my cousin, James Alden, and his delightful grandchildren, Henry, Jessie, Violet, and Benny Alden."

Jessie smiled and put out her hand for a handshake. "Oh, someone at the general store mentioned your name," she said.

Mr. Mason didn't smile back, shake hands, or seem the least bit interested in Jessie or any of the Aldens.

"I guess we'll have to finish our business some other time, Charlotte," he finally said before opening the garden gate to leave. "I see you're too busy with all these people to discuss business right now."

Cousin Charlotte didn't let this stop her. "Actually, I'm glad you're here, William. When I heard my cousin was driving up this way on business, I asked him to bring along the children to help at Skeleton Point, too. I'd like nothing better than to have you work with them. There are so many things they can do."

Mr. Mason stared at Charlotte before he finally spoke. "Well, if children are involved, I'm not sure you need a trained architect like me. I'll see you in the morning to discuss these plans. Good day."

Before Charlotte could say another word, Mr. Mason headed down the street.

Grandfather gave Cousin Charlotte a

hug. "I'm sorry if we interrupted something important."

Charlotte gave the children the same welcoming Alden smile Grandfather often gave his grandchildren. "Not to worry, James. William and I were just winding up when you arrived. After he read in the paper that I had bought Skeleton Point, he contacted me to see if I needed help. I'm very lucky to have him, since he's a retired architect. He specialized in old buildings."

Benny could hardly stand still now that he had something exciting to tell Charlotte. "How about old skeletons?" he asked. "He'd better like those when he's at Skeleton Point, 'cause, know what? That's what's out there. We saw a real skeleton staring out the window and a hairy monster in the lake."

Charlotte's soft blue eyes widened in surprise. "Goodness, something in the lake, too? The one you saw in the window is Mister Bones. Sorry if he gave you a scare," Charlotte told the children. "I left him hanging there to keep trespassers away from the house, just like Dr. Tibbs used to do. But I didn't think there was a *monster* in the lake." Cousin Charlotte laughed. "What did it look like?"

Jessie explained about the T-shirt Henry had found on the porch railing and the swimmer with the long hair.

"Don't forget the barking dog," Benny reminded Jessie.

Charlotte chuckled. "Oh, that was probably Greeny Owen's dog, Max. And Greeny himself was the swimmer, most likely. He was once a student of Dr. Tibbs. He never did finish medical school, but he knows more about bones than most doctors. Local people have told me he's quite upset that I bought the property. Over the years, he's come to think of it as his. He works in a lab at the medical school and often swims or rows over from the island, where he lives with Max."

"Does he have lots of hair?" Benny wanted to know.

"Well, Max has short hair, and Greeny has long hair — for a man, that is," Charlotte explained. "Plus a little skull earring. He often wears that black T-shirt with the skull and skeleton on it. He must have taken it off to go swimming. Nobody but Greeny would go swimming on such a damp, chilly day."

"He didn't scare us." Benny felt brave now that he had arrived at Charlotte's cozy house. "Not a bit."

Charlotte hugged Benny, then gave each of the other children a hug, too. "Well, I'm glad of that. I can't seem to make a friend of Greeny yet. I'm hoping you children will have better luck. He knows so much about Dr. Tibbs's skeleton collection. I'd love to ask him to organize it before I send it on to the medical school. Unfortunately, he disappears on me whenever I go over to Skeleton Point."

"That's what he did with us," Henry said. "Disappeared right under the water."

As Charlotte led the children to a greenhouse in back of her house, she told the children more about Greeny. "I suppose I should be glad that he and Max do such a good job of guarding the property. The problem is, he chases off everyone, including the locksmith I sent over last week! Maybe the four of you will have better luck getting to know him and Max."

"We like dogs," Jessie said. "Especially watchdogs. Our dog, Watch, guarded us when we lived in a boxcar we fixed up in the woods after our mother and father died. Now Watch watches out for us at Grandfather's house."

Charlotte put her arm around Jessie. "I'm so glad Watch — and Cousin James — found you. Now, here's another house for you to live in while you're here — my old greenhouse. I didn't need all of it for plants, so I turned the rest of it into a guest cottage. See?"

"Oh." Violet was so pleased when she walked into the all-glass building, she hardly knew what to say. "We'll be able to see the stars and moon at night."

"And the moon and stars will be able to see you — at least when this foggy weather blows away." Charlotte led the children to the far end of the greenhouse. "You can put your sleeping bags down on these camp cots. You're also welcome to sleep out at Skeleton Point anytime. There are several decent beds in the tower of the house. Just bring your sleeping bags."

"Too bad the rest of us have to sleep in a house with a roof you can't see through," Grandfather joked. "You've done a wonderful job with this greenhouse, Charlotte. We certainly spent a lot of happy hours in here when we were children. Now it's my grandchildren's turn to have some fun in here."

"I hope so," Charlotte said. "Now come inside my real house for some cookies and lemonade. You children must be starving."

"I sure am," Benny said as if he had completely forgotten the ice-cream cone he'd polished off just a little while before.

The children followed Charlotte through the back garden and into her kitchen. Just as everyone sat down, the phone rang.

"Help yourselves," Charlotte said before she went to answer it.

The children passed around a basket of

oatmeal cookies. While they munched, they could hear Charlotte speaking with someone about Skeleton Point and the Aldens.

"You'll love Cousin James's grandchildren," they heard Charlotte say. "They are very grown-up and love hard work. They once fixed up an old boxcar in the woods and lived in it."

Charlotte looked a bit more thoughtful when she returned. "Sorry I took so long. That was Hilda Stone. She's an artist who just opened a studio in Shady Lake. William hired her to assist with the artworks that came with the Skeleton Point property," Charlotte said. "I must say, the two of them have some very definite opinions about the work out there and how it should be done. Sometimes they forget that I'm the owner!"

"Violet's an artist, too," Henry said. "If you need any drawings or pictures, Violet's the one to ask."

Charlotte nodded. "That's just what your grandfather told me on the phone. I'd love to have you children photograph and draw some of the artworks at Skeleton Point so

I can have some before-and-after pictures. The statues are just crumbling to pieces, especially lately. That's how all the Walking Skeleton stories got started."

Benny put down his cookie. "A lady at the general store said the Walking Skeleton takes arms and hands from the statues so it can turn into a person again!"

"That's one of the tales going around, but, of course, it's just a story," Charlotte said. "I really don't know how the statues got damaged recently. They are quite old and already worn away by the weather. But now a few pieces are missing — not just falling off, but disappearing. I do hope you can all keep an eye on the property."

This gave Jessie a good idea. "We gave Benny an instant camera for his birthday. If we take pictures of the statues and something happens to them, maybe we can figure out when it happened and who was around at that time."

"Excellent," Charlotte said. "I'll be dropping off a job list tomorrow morning with Hilda and William. I'll make sure to tell them to let you children photograph and sketch around the property. That will give them more time to do other things."

"Here's to catching the Walking Skeleton!" Jessie said.

The Aldens clinked their lemonade glasses.

CHAPTER 3

Skullduggery

By the time the Alden children tucked themselves into bed in the greenhouse, a steady breeze was blowing in from Shady Lake. The children gazed up through the glass ceiling and walls. Branches on Charlotte's willow tree gently swayed back and forth, back and forth. Soon all four children were sound asleep.

But they did not sleep through the night. At four in the morning, a crack of thunder shook the greenhouse. Seconds later, streaks of lightning lit it up.

Jessie sat up first, after she heard some barking. "Watch!" she said, when she thought she saw a dog outside the greenhouse. She rubbed her eyes. "Oh, we're at Charlotte's, not at home."

Soon loud plops of rain pelted the greenhouse.

Henry pulled his pillow around his ears. "What a racket!"

Benny scrunched himself way down into his sleeping bag. "Make the noise go away."

Violet leaned over from her cot and patted Benny. "They're only raindrops. Oh, no, what's that?" Violet asked when she saw something move outside the greenhouse.

By the time Jessie looked out, the lightning was over and everything was completely dark again. "I think the lightning played tricks on our eyes. We'd better go back to sleep."

The noisy raindrops gave way to a gentle rain, and everyone fell asleep again. An hour and a half later, the greenhouse filled with light.

"It's only five-thirty," Henry said when he

checked his watch. "It's so bright in here."

Jessie yawned and stretched. "I dreamed Violet saw somebody with a dog outside during the storm. I thought Watch had followed us to Shady Lake."

The Aldens quickly dressed and rolled up their sleeping bags. They had a big day ahead.

Charlotte was enjoying a cup of coffee with Grandfather when the children entered the kitchen. "Good morning," Charlotte said, passing around a basket of blueberry muffins. "Take as many as you like," she told the children. "Cousin James said you brought your bikes with you and want to bike out to Skeleton Point today instead of having us drive you there. It's several miles each way on the bike path. You're welcome to take out my rowboat, too. It's the yellow one tied to the dock below Skeleton Point. You're going to need a lot of energy for all your activities, so eat up."

"We will," Henry said as he buttered his muffin. "Are you and Grandfather going to come with us?"

"Not today, children," Grandfather answered. "Charlotte and I have another cousin who lives upstate. She's been feeling poorly, so we're leaving for a few days, after Charlotte stops off at Skeleton Point."

Charlotte put down her cup. "I'm going to meet with William and Hilda on the way. I'll tell them I want you children to photograph and sketch the gardens and the house inside and out."

After the children made their lunches, they went to get their bikes in Charlotte's toolshed. That's when they got an awful shock.

"What's this?" Henry asked when he pulled his helmet from his bike bag. "Did you guys play a trick on me?" Inside Henry's helmet, a plastic Halloween skull grinned back at him.

"Hey! There's a skull in my bike helmet, too! And in yours and yours," Benny said, pointing to the grinning plastic skulls inside his sisters' helmets. "Somebody played a joke, but it wasn't me."

When Charlotte came out, she didn't find

the joke quite as funny, though she tried to laugh about it. "Goodness. I guess I can always use them at Halloween for my trick-or-treaters."

Benny turned one of the skulls upside down to see if anything was inside. "We got the trick but not the treat."

Charlotte laughed. "Well, if you children need more treats than what I left out for your lunches, stop at the general store. The bike path runs right behind it. You'll see a sign for it."

"Goody," Benny said. "I saw lots of snacks there yesterday."

The children put on their helmets and set off for the bike path. Since it was still early, they had it to themselves for a while.

Jessie checked the small bike mirror on her handlebars and saw a jogger in the distance. "I guess runners use this path, too," she told the others. "There's somebody behind us."

When Henry turned around to take a look, the jogger took off into the woods. "Whoever it was is gone."

The children rolled along, making good time on the smooth, empty path.

"There's the sign for the general store. Should we stop?" Jessie teased, even though she already knew the answer.

"I saw gorp fixings in the store — nuts, raisins, and chocolate chips," Henry said.

"Good, gorp," Benny said about the delicious, healthy snack they often brought on their outings.

The general store was already busy with people buying fishing tackle, getting mail, drinking coffee, and picking up groceries and the morning newspaper.

Jessie led the way to the camping section. "Here are the nuts and raisins. Benny, you and Violet go over to the baking aisle for the chips. I brought along some zip bags so we can mix up some gorp for each of us."

When Benny and Violet came to the next aisle, a young woman was blocking the way. She and one of the cardplayers the children had seen the day before were so busy talking, they didn't see the children standing there.

"Have you lived here a very long time?" the young woman asked the man, who was wearing a fishing vest today. "I'm trying to get information about those statues out at Skeleton Point. Nobody seems to know how old they are or where they came from."

"Or where some parts of the statues are going," the man told the young woman. "Lots of fool stories are going around about somebody — or something — damaging the statues. Stay away from them, I say. Those old statues have been out there forever — before I was born, anyway. Leave 'em be. Why do you want to know?"

The young woman hesitated, then stopped to read the label on a jar of honey. "Um . . . just curious."

With that, the young woman left the store without buying anything.

"Newcomers!" the man told Benny and Violet when he saw them standing there. "Always asking questions. You'd think from that young lady that Shady Lake was nothing but old statues covered with moss. What about our fishing? Why, our trout are practically jumping out of the lake."

"They are?" Benny asked, hoping to find out where he could see some of these jumping trout.

The man left without answering Benny.

"All set?" Jessie said when she and Henry joined the younger children. "Let's go pay for everything."

While the children stood in line, they heard a grinding sound nearby. One of the clerks was making keys for a customer. "Here's the extra key you wanted, Greeny." The worker handed over a new key and a brown bag. "Bring it back if it doesn't fit this lock you just bought."

"That must be Greeny Owen!" Henry whispered to his brother and sisters.

"I guess even on the island you have to be careful to keep your cabin locked up, huh?" the clerk asked.

"Um . . . right." Greeny pocketed the key and put the bag in the small backpack he wore over his T-shirt and jogging shorts. He stepped away from the counter and left.

"I think Greeny was the jogger I saw in my bike mirror," Jessie said quietly.

Henry agreed. "I bet you're right. I wonder why he ran into the woods when I turned around. It was almost like he was following us but didn't want us to see him."

After the children made up their gorp bags, they returned to the parking lot.

Benny poked Henry, then Jessie. "See that lady getting in the red car? She was being nosy about the statues when she was talking to that fisherman," Benny said.

Henry watched the woman back out her red car and head down the road. "There sure are a lot of people besides Charlotte interested in those statues."

CHAPTER 4

The Aldens Have a Dog Day

After a long bike ride, the Aldens finally came to Skeleton Point. Just as the children slowed down, a familiar dog bounded from the bushes and barked. Then he began to sniff around.

"He smells our ham sandwiches," Benny guessed.

"There, there, Max," Jessie said softly.

The dog tilted his head the way Watch always did when someone knew his name and spoke gently to him.

Jessie carefully reached into her bike bag.

She found her ham sandwich and tossed a piece of it to Max. This calmed him right away. When the dog whined for more, Jessie tossed another piece farther off. The children didn't have to worry about the dog now.

"I'm glad that worked," Jessie said. "I wonder if Greeny knows his dog is loose."

The next thing the children heard was somebody yelling and whistling. "Max! Maxilla! Get over here!"

"What kind of a name is Maxilla?" Benny wanted to know.

Henry laughed. "It's part of a jawbone. I guess it's a good name for a dog whose owner wears a skull shirt."

"Max!" the children heard again. This time the dog dashed off into the woods to join Greeny.

A few minutes later, when the children rounded the point, they saw Max and Greeny about to get into a rowboat. Then Greeny disappeared into some trees and returned with a blue milk crate. That, too, went into the boat. He whistled for Max to jump in. Soon he and Max headed out to an island a short distance from shore.

"I wonder why he docked at Skeleton Point instead of closer to the general store," Henry said. "From the looks of it, that milk crate seemed pretty heavy."

Jessie wondered the same thing. "Do you think it came from Skeleton Point?"

Violet didn't want to believe anything bad about Greeny. "Maybe he had some personal things he had left with Dr. Tibbs and came by to get them back."

"There's only one way to find out," Henry said. "We'll have to keep an eye on Greeny Owen."

A few minutes later, Henry pulled his bike off the path. "We'll never get our bikes up these steps. Let's tie them up to some trees."

After the children locked their bikes, they began their climb up the wooden steps that went to the top of Skeleton Point.

"Hey, look, there's a shortcut off this path," Benny said when the children had gone halfway. "Can we see where it goes?"

"Sure," Henry said. "After you."

When he came to a small clearing at the far end of the overgrown gardens, Benny spotted someone up ahead sitting on a rock. "Who's that?"

The children walked toward the person.

"Maybe it's Hilda Stone," Violet said. "I hope so. I'd like to meet a real artist."

Something seemed odd to Jessie. "It's funny that person doesn't hear us and turn around. Hello!" she called out. "We're here."

"She's as still as a statue," Violet whispered.

Benny ran ahead. "It *is* a statue — of a girl sitting on a rock," he said. "We sure got fooled."

Violet went up to the statue. The small figure seemed to be gazing at the lake. "She looks so sad. I wonder who it's supposed to be. This one isn't broken like the others." Violet walked around the statue, studying it from every side. "There's a name carved on the back: *Clover Dodge*."

"Can I take a picture of you next to it?" Benny asked Violet.

"Sure." Violet sat next to the statue. "That's what we planned to do anyway. Later I want to sketch this one. It's beautiful."

"Say cheese," Benny said, but Violet just sat peacefully looking out at the lake, not thinking of cheese at all.

A few minutes later, the children huddled around Benny to wait for the instant picture to appear.

"Oh, it's so beautiful," Jessie said to Violet. "I wonder who Clover Dodge was."

The children walked toward the house. Along the way, they posed next to some of the other statues.

"Hey, my camera's stuck!" Benny complained when he aimed it at Henry, who was imitating the stone lion near the house.

Jessie came over to take a look. "That's because you're out of film, silly. Let's go inside. By now Charlotte must have dropped off the job list. I don't see any cars, but maybe William and Hilda parked by the road."

This time, when they passed Mister Bones in the window, the children waved at

him as if they were used to seeing full-sized skeletons every day.

"Hi, Mister Bones," Benny said. "I'll have to take your picture another time."

Inside, the whole house seemed to creak with every step the children took.

Henry led the way. "Ugh. What was that?" he asked when something brushed against his face. "I hope it wasn't a bat."

The children looked up.

"Eew, it's a long, dusty cobweb," Jessie said.

The children crept along, trying not to walk into any more sticky cobwebs. They soon found the room with Mister Bones hanging in the window. Every corner of Dr. Tibbs's study was full of all kinds of skeletons and skulls — little mouse skulls, the skull from a horse, and many bird and animal skeletons of different sizes.

Violet went over to a delicate bird skeleton.

"Don't even think of touching that," a voice said.

The children whirled around. In the

Jessie sat up first, after she heard some barking. "Watch!" she said, when she thought she saw a dog outside the greenhouse. She rubbed her eyes. "Oh, we're at Charlotte's, not at home."

Soon loud plops of rain pelted the greenhouse.

Henry pulled his pillow around his ears. "What a racket!"

Benny scrunched himself way down into his sleeping bag. "Make the noise go away."

Violet leaned over from her cot and patted Benny. "They're only raindrops. Oh, no, what's that?" Violet asked when she saw something move outside the greenhouse.

By the time Jessie looked out, the lightning was over and everything was completely dark again. "I think the lightning played tricks on our eyes. We'd better go back to sleep."

The noisy raindrops gave way to a gentle rain, and everyone fell asleep again. An hour and a half later, the greenhouse filled with light.

"It's only five-thirty," Henry said when he

olet, plus my brother, Benny. Charlotte asked us to help out, just like you."

Hilda Stone took a long time before speaking. "Well, William Mason hired me because I'm a trained artist. A historical house, with so many art treasures, requires experts, not children running about."

Benny felt brave even though Hilda Stone was a little bit scarier than Mr. Bones. "We weren't running. We took our bikes, then we walked up the path, nice and quiet. Plus, I took pictures of all the statues with my camera."

Henry nudged Benny so he wouldn't say anything more. "What Benny means is we'd like to give Charlotte pictures of the property so she knows what has to be fixed."

Footsteps on the squeaky floors interrupted Henry. A long shadow fell across the floor. "That's hardly something for children to decide," a deep voice said.

Even Hilda Stone jumped back. "William! Goodness, I didn't know you were in the house."

William Mason stepped into the room.

"Been here for an hour. Charlotte stopped by and left us a list of chores to finish before she gets back in a few days."

"Us?" Hilda asked. "Does that mean just you and me or these kids, too?"

"All of us," Jessie said in her own clear voice. "Remember, she told you on the phone that she was sending us out here to work? She told Mr. Mason the same thing. That's why we're here."

Mr. Mason looked down at the paper in his hand. "Well, I'm here because I'm an architect. Hilda is here because she's an artist. Yes, we can certainly put you to work. Why don't you go outside and wait? Hilda and I will discuss how to proceed."

"She's the same lady who was asking all those questions in the store," Benny told Jessie when they went outside. "Only we didn't know she was Charlotte's friend. How come she's not friendly?"

Henry put his arm around Benny. "Don't worry about Hilda. We'll just have to get to know her, I guess. Maybe she'll be friendlier when she sees how hard we work."

But it looked like Henry might be wrong. When Hilda came out to speak with the children, she wasn't at all friendly. "William and I need you to go over to the hardware store across the lake for some special light switches," Hilda told the Aldens. "We're too busy right now to drive there."

Henry thought about this. "That'll take a pretty long time, since we're on bikes. Wouldn't it be faster to go in the car so we can all get started working around here?"

Hilda shook her head. "As I said, we simply don't have time to run errands today. Charlotte told William that you know how to row a boat. Her rowboat is the yellow one down by the dock. Here's the combination for the lock. There are enough life jackets below the seats. Row straight past the island to the buildings on the other side of the lake. One of them is the hardware store. Ask for the owner, Brad."

"Sure thing," Henry said when Hilda handed him the information on a piece of paper. "How do we pay for the switches?"

"Well . . . tell Brad to put the bill on Charlotte's account."

Henry had one more thing to say. "Charlotte said maybe Violet could sketch some of the statues out there — before-and-after pictures, so people can see how Skeleton Point used to be."

Hilda had other plans. "No need for that. William and I have already taken note of the outdoor sculptures. Professionals examine artwork in certain ways."

Violet, who hadn't said very much, spoke up now. "We'd love to learn to do that — if you could teach us, that is."

For a second, Hilda seemed almost interested in Violet's request. Then she looked back at the house. William was on the porch waving for her to come inside. She turned back to Violet. "No, no, I haven't time to teach you children my methods. There's so much else to be done. Right now we need those light switches. As for the statues, they are quite fragile. We can't have you working around them in any way."

CHAPTER 5

A Forbidden Island

The children rowed along, enjoying the lake, the birds flying overhead, and the nice easy sound of the lake lapping against the boat.

"I have to admit, this is kind of fun," Jessie said as she pulled the oars of Charlotte's yellow rowboat through the clear water. "We haven't been rowing for a long time. Make sure to tell me if I'm rowing in the right direction."

Benny, face-to-face with Jessie, gave her directions. "If you go straight, you'll bump

into that island where Greeny lives. I wish we could go there, but he might get mad at us."

Henry scanned the lake with the binoculars. "You're right about that, Benny. Not to mention he'd probably send Max after us."

"May I have the binoculars, Henry?" Violet asked. "I'd like to see what Greeny's house looks like." She soon spotted a small log cabin nestled between some trees. "The island is pretty," she said, "but lonely-looking, too. I wonder what it's like to live out there with no family."

"We'll be passing close by," Henry said. "Maybe we can get a look."

Benny took a turn with the binoculars, too. "Hey! A seal is swimming to our boat!"

The older children laughed.

"Benny!" Henry said. "Seals don't live in freshwater lakes. They're ocean mammals. Maybe it's one of those jumping trout you wanted to see."

Benny handed Henry the binoculars. "Take a look. Something furry, not fishy, is swimming around."

"You know what, Benny? You're right," Henry said, surprised. "I do see a furry head swimming our way. Jessie, row slightly to your right, toward the island."

A few strokes later, Benny's "seal" was so close to the boat, the Aldens saw right away that it was Max.

"Max!" Violet called out. "Come here, boy. It's your friends, the Aldens. Come on, Maxilla!"

Jessie rowed carefully. "I'll get closer to the island," she told her brothers and sister. "I know Labs are good swimmers, but I don't want Max to swim out too far. He might get tired."

Max looked far from being tired. He kept his head well above the water and paddled at a nice steady pace. Pretty soon he was alongside the Aldens' boat.

Benny reached down to pat Max's wet head. "Good boy."

The children heard a loud whistle in the air.

"Yo! Maxilla, get back here!"

"It's Greeny." Henry made a megaphone

out of his hands so Greeny would hear him. "Is it okay to come to shore?"

Greeny yelled back, "I guess so. Otherwise Max'll never come in. Pull up on the beach in front of the flagpole." He then went over to his own boat and covered it with a sheet of canvas.

"Darn!" Henry said. "Now we won't be able to see what was in that milk crate he picked up at Skeleton Point."

Jessie guided the rowboat toward the small, stony beach. Max swam alongside so closely the Aldens could see his four legs paddling through the water in a real dog-paddle stroke!

When the boat glided to the beach, Greeny grabbed the rope hooked to the bow. "Pull up here."

Once he got ashore, Max yipped and barked the way Watch always did after a good swim. The Aldens stood back. They knew very well that when Max shook out his fur, they were in for a big shower.

"We wanted to come here," Violet said, "but we didn't know if you liked company. I guess Max came out to invite us."

"Max and I don't get much company out this way," Greeny told the Aldens. "I figured you kids would be busy at the house with those other people poking around Skeleton Point. Did those two friends of Charlotte chase you away, too?"

"You mean William and Hilda?" Jessie asked. "Well, we thought you and Max were chasing *us* away by scaring us when we went looking around yesterday. We heard somebody say, 'What are *you* doing here?' "

Greeny looked away from the children. "Well, I thought you were trespassers, so I gave you a little scare. There've been problems out there lately."

"Did we scare you off the bike path this morning?" Violet asked, softly.

Greeny looked away and didn't answer.

The Aldens didn't find him scary now in his bright red T-shirt and jogging shorts. Even his skull earring looked like the ones Jessie wore on Halloween. His long hair was tied in a neat ponytail.

"I wasn't scared of you," Greeny told the

children. "I'm just not feeling too friendly toward a bunch of strangers taking over Doc Tibbs's place."

Jessie took a deep breath before she spoke. "It's Charlotte's place now. She's fixing it up."

Greeny's mouth tightened. "It doesn't need fixing up any more than the woods need fixing up. Doc's skeleton collection is one of the most important ones in the country. He taught hundreds of medical and veterinary students. Now people are just going in there, moving things around, and even taking things from his collection."

"Some were stolen?" Violet asked. "We looked at some of the bird and animal skeletons, but we wouldn't touch anything without permission."

This didn't cheer up Greeny at all. "Nobody around here knows enough about skeletons to give anyone permission to look at the skeletons."

"You know enough," Violet said in her quiet way. "Charlotte hopes you'll help organize Dr. Tibbs's collection before she donates it to the medical school where it belongs. She says you always run away from her."

Greeny stroked Max's head while he thought about this. "That's because she acts like she owns Skeleton Point and everything in it."

"Well, she does," Jessie reminded Greeny. "But she wants the collection to be kept together and go to the right place."

Greeny got worked up all over again when he heard this. "The right place was to me. But Doc up and died before he wrote out his will. He told me he was leaving me his collection so I could decide what to do with it. Then Charlotte went and bought the place."

"I bet you didn't know she's using all her savings to fix up everything — the house, the statues, and the gardens," Jessie said. "Charlotte really cares about Skeleton Point."

"Well, so do I," Greeny said. "I've kept a watch on it better than anybody. If it weren't for Max and me, the place would be in worse shape than it is. All this hullabaloo about Walking Skeletons and such — those are just stories to cover up plain old thievery and vandalism."

"What's vandalism?" Benny wanted to know.

"People harming property," Jessie said. "Like Charlotte's statues. She bought them, so they belong to her now."

Greeny disagreed with Jessie. "Those statues were priceless — they can't just be bought." Greeny was finished with the Aldens. "Now I think you should get going. I can see we're never going to see eye to eye on this, that's for sure."

The children walked back to the shore. Henry and Jessie dragged the boat to the water's edge. The children climbed in.

" 'Bye, Greeny," Benny yelled as Henry dipped the oars in the water. " 'Bye, Max."

When the children looked back at the island, they heard Max bark to say good-bye, but Greeny had disappeared into his cabin.

Henry rowed the next leg of the trip

across Shady Lake. The other shore soon came into view. "I can't decide about Greeny," Henry said. "He doesn't seem to think anybody has a right to be at Skeleton Point but him."

Violet, who was trailing her hand in the water, had a soft spot for Greeny. "He just wants to protect the property, I think. Let's try to make friends with him. I just know if we do, he'll help Charlotte."

"That's a very sensible idea, Violet," Jessie said. "The better we get to know him, the better our chances are of finding out who's harming Charlotte's property."

Henry finally reached the small marina. "There's the hardware store Hilda told us about," he said. "We'd better pick up those light switches and get back. We lost a lot of time stopping off to see Greeny."

When the children entered the hardware store, they found the owner at the cash register.

Henry handed the man the piece of paper Hilda had given him. "I hope you're

Brad. Hilda Stone told us to see you about some special light switches. They're for the lights over at Skeleton Point."

"I am Brad," the man said, "but I have no idea what you're talking about, young fellow. I don't carry these light switches and never did. And who's this Hilda Stone person, anyway? Probably one of these city people buying up property who doesn't know a darn thing about what she's doing. Never heard of her."

The Aldens looked at one another. Hadn't Hilda told them to find Brad and pick up the special switches?

"What about William Mason?" Jessie thought to ask. "Do you know him?"

"Who doesn't know William Mason?" the man asked. "I'm surprised he volunteered to help fix up that old house. Mason's a fellow who's always trying to make a buck or two. In fact, now that I think about it, he did some talking about wanting to buy the house himself, but Charlotte beat him to it. Doesn't stop him from walking around like he owns the place."

"He does?" Benny asked. "I thought Greeny Owen was the only one who acted like that."

"Greeny?" the man said. "There's another one always creeping around these old places on the lake. Don't know which is worse, the newcomers or the old-timers who think everything on the lake should stay the same as it was a hundred years ago. That's Greeny for you. Sorry about the light switches. You need to go to one of the big stores over in North River for those. It was a total waste of time sending you here."

CHAPTER 6

The Hidden Trail

When the children returned to the dock empty-handed, they got a terrible surprise.

"Our boat is floating away!" Jessie pointed to their little yellow rowboat bobbing out on the lake about twenty feet away. "How did that happen? I know I tied it up."

"Wait here," Henry told Violet and Benny. "We're going to swim after it."

In a flash, Henry and Jessie stripped down to their bathing suits and plunged into the water. They were excellent swimmers and reached the boat in no time.

"Whew," Henry said when he caught his breath — and the boat. "That was close. Thank goodness the wind wasn't blowing any harder. The boat didn't get out too far. You climb in, Jessie. I'll swim along while you row back."

"I wonder how the boat got loose," Jessie said when she and Henry reached the dock.

Jessie got out of the boat and walked over to join Violet and Benny, who were talking to a fisherman on the dock. "Somebody let your boat go," said the fisherman. "A fellow was trying to untie his motorboat, but he unlocked yours by mistake. Guess he forgot to lock yours back up again. I tried calling after him, but he just sped right off. Folks can be mighty careless sometimes."

"Which way did he go?" asked Jessie. The fisherman pointed across the lake toward Skeleton Point.

Jessie reached for the binoculars to take a look. She spotted a motorboat heading out. "Look out there." She handed Henry the binoculars. "Doesn't that look like Mr. Mason from behind?"

Henry grabbed the glasses. "I think it is him. I recognize the red hat he had on yesterday. If he had a motorboat, why did Hilda tell us they didn't have time to go to the hardware store?"

Jessie found the towel she'd packed and shared it with Henry. "The sun will have to dry off the rest of us," she said. "If you ask me, those two are trying to keep us away from Cousin Charlotte's property."

"Well, they can't," Henry said. "Hop in, everybody. We're going to follow Mr. Mason back to Skeleton Point."

But Henry couldn't follow the motorboat to Skeleton Point. It sped right past there without stopping.

"He must be docking someplace else," Jessie said. "That gives me an idea. Instead of going back to Skeleton Point, let's row to that cove we passed not too far from the general store. We'll hike up from there. If Hilda and William don't spot our boat coming in, we'll have a chance to see what they're up to before they expect us back."

Henry didn't need to think twice about Jessie's good suggestion. He dipped one oar into the water and headed for the deserted cove.

After they pulled up, the children dragged the boat as far onto shore as they could.

The woods were still as the Aldens crept along. They soon came to a broken fence that surrounded Skeleton Point.

"Let's go in this way," Henry said when he and Jessie found an opening. "I think I see a trail on the other side."

Once the children were on the property again, they followed the overgrown path that curved around the hillside. With Jessie leading the way, the children hiked single file, holding branches back for one another.

Violet bumped into Jessie when she suddenly stopped. "What's the matter, Jessie?" Violet asked. "Are we at the end?"

Jessie pointed to a rock up ahead. "Come see this rock face. Doesn't it look like a skull, especially with the way there's some old paint where the eyes and mouth are?"

Henry examined the rock. He found a rusted metal door blocking a wide crack in the rock. The door didn't budge. "This is getting weirder and weirder. It's some kind of cave that somebody put a door on. By the looks of it, it's been here a long time. Let's see where this trail goes. I have a feeling it joins up with that other shortcut we took off the main path."

When Violet and Benny stopped for a drink from their water bottles, Jessie pulled Henry aside. "I didn't want to scare Violet and Benny, but I saw something moving up ahead. It could have been a deer, I suppose. Whatever it was, it ran off in the direction we're going."

"Uh-oh," Henry said. "Here comes Benny. I wonder if he saw it, too."

"There's a big skull up there — a real one! See?" Benny pointed to a horse skull stuck in the notch of a tree right by the footpath.

"Somebody's playing a trick," Jessie said so the younger children wouldn't get too

scared. "Let's leave it there so no one knows we saw it."

Benny liked this idea. "Nobody can scare us away, right, Jessie?"

"Right."

Benny and Violet finished drinking their water. They stayed close to Henry and Jessie. Soon the trail crossed the main path between the beach and the house.

"Let's pick it up on the other side," Henry suggested. "Hilda and William won't expect us from that direction."

"This leads to the garden where the Clover Dodge statue is," Violet said.

But Violet was mistaken. "The statue is gone!" she said when she came to the rock where it had been anchored. "Should we go tell Hilda and William?"

Jessie and Henry exchanged glances.

"Let's see if they tell us first," Jessie suggested. "Maybe they had a good reason to take it. And if they didn't, I don't want them to know right away that we know it's missing. I'd also like to find out who made these fresh footprints."

The children looked down at the ground where the statue had been.

"Whoever was here had on work boots or hiking boots with thick treads on the soles." Henry checked his watch. "We've been gone a long time. Hilda and William will be looking for us. Let's look for them first."

The children hiked through the surrounding woods so they could watch the house without being seen. No one seemed to be around until they approached the empty reflecting pool.

Jessie put her finger to her lips. "Shhh. Stop here. Don't breathe."

They watched Hilda Stone go from statue to statue with a sketch pad and a measuring tape. At every statue, she stopped, measured parts of the statues, then marked something down. When she was done, she returned to the house.

The children backtracked to the steps. They'd gone partway up when Benny stopped suddenly.

There was a full-sized seated skeleton in

front of them on the steps. "The Walking Skeleton!" Benny said.

Henry chuckled. "No, I guess you'd have to call it the Sitting Skeleton. It's just sitting there as if it stopped to take a rest."

"I'm not afraid of Halloween tricks even when it's not Halloween." Benny scurried past the skeleton.

Henry looked very serious. "Now I know someone is trying to scare us away from Skeleton Point again," he said.

"You're probably right, Henry," said Jessie. "But who could it be?"

"William Mason and Hilda Stone," said Benny, almost immediately. "They're mean to us, and they don't want us around."

"You're right, Benny. Remember that man in town said William Mason wanted to buy Skeleton Point for himself? Maybe he's mad at Charlotte for buying it first."

Jessie looked thoughtful. "What about Greeny?" she asked. "We know he doesn't want us around, either — and we know he's taking things from the house. Maybe he wants to scare us away so we won't figure out what he's up to. We should still keep an eye on him."

Henry agreed. "In fact, we should keep an eye on all of them."

When they returned to the house, the Aldens found that William had joined Hilda outside.

Jessie waved. "Hi!" she called out, as if she had come straight from her errand across the lake. "Sorry we took so long. The hardware store was out of those light switches."

Hilda and William kept working. It seemed neither of them wanted to say anything.

Finally Hilda spoke up. "Oh, it turns out we don't need them after all."

William pushed back the brim of his red hat and checked his watch. "Half the day's gone. I don't see much use for you kids sticking around here. Hilda and I are doing some technical work Charlotte asked us to do — not something suitable for children."

"We know how to measure, too" Benny said. "I learned in kindergarten."

Hilda hesitated. "What we're doing is a little more complicated than what you do in school. Now, why don't you children go for a bike ride. Or a swim," she suggested before going into the house.

Henry turned to William. "We already went for a swim," he said. "An unplanned one."

William didn't say anything about untying the Aldens' boat, but he looked away and cleared his throat. "Well, then, go for a planned one this afternoon. Take tomorrow off, too. Everything's under control here."

Before William turned to go into the house, the Aldens looked down. Just as they suspected, William was wearing heavy work boots that left deep prints just like the ones near the statue.

CHAPTER 7

The Secret in the Library

After breakfast the next morning, the Aldens made their lunches in Cousin Charlotte's kitchen. While they were bagging their lunches, the phone rang.

Jessie ran for it, and the other children listened in. "Cousin Charlotte! We're fine. We just got our lunches and extra food ready before we leave for town. Then we're riding to Skeleton Point. We're even going to spend the night since you said it was okay." Jessie handed the phone to Henry.

"No, William and Hilda haven't told us

what we'll be doing next," Henry said. "All we did yesterday was run an errand, then we biked home.

Charlotte told them all about her trip with Grandfather. Then she added something surprising. "Before we left yesterday, we came across a plastic skeleton — right by the car!"

"You came across a skeleton yesterday, too? So did we!" Henry said.

After that, the younger children took turns speaking with Cousin Charlotte and Grandfather about some of their adventures the day before. By the time they hung up, they were nearly out of breath.

Henry handed the other children their lunches. "Cousin Charlotte's going to tell William to let us into Dr. Tibbs's study this afternoon. She wants us to count everything so she knows exactly what's there before she sends it to the medical school."

"What about the missing statue?" Violet asked. "Did you mention it to her?"

Henry's face grew serious. "I didn't have the heart to tell her about that yet. I was thinking we could bike to town and visit Hilda's studio. Without William around, maybe she'll tell us what she knows about the statues. So what do you say, guys? Everybody ready?"

Ten minutes later, the children headed into town, biking carefully now that their bikes were loaded down with their sleeping bags and overnight things. They parked their bikes in front of the drugstore to pick up film for Benny.

Benny unzipped his bike bag to get his camera. "Hey, my pictures aren't in here with my camera. They were in my bike bag yesterday."

"Are you sure?" Jessie asked Benny. "Did you leave it unzipped? I hope the pictures didn't fall out while we were biking."

Benny shook his head. "No way. I zipped everything up. Remember? I left the bike bag on the porch when we went out in the boat and picked it up when we got back."

Jessie had a suggestion. "Then the pictures must be out at Skeleton Point. We'll look around when we go there this afternoon."

While Jessie ran into the drugstore to get the film, Henry took out the map Charlotte had given him. "Hilda's studio is the next block over," he said when Jessie came out again. "Let's go see if she's there."

When the children rang Hilda's bell, no one answered. A sign with an arrow pointing to the back of the house read, STUDIO. The children walked along quietly, looking in the windows of the house to see if anyone was around. A sign on the garage door read, STUDIO CLOSED.

Jessie cupped her hands over the tall windows of the studio. Then she waved for the other children to come over and look inside, too.

"The Clover Dodge statue!" Violet whispered when she peeked in.

Hilda was seated at a cluttered worktable facing away from the Aldens. The statue stood in the middle of the table. Also on the table were a life-sized skull and a skeleton of a hand. Hilda was bent over a large drawing pad, sketching a large stone arm that looked familiar to the Aldens.

The children tiptoed away.

"We have to decide what to do next," Jessie said.

"A book I noticed on a shelf in the studio gave me an idea," Violet said. "The title was, *Sculptures of Clover Dodge*. It must be the name of the sculptor who made the statue. My idea is to go to the library and see if we can find out more about Clover Dodge."

"Good thinking," Henry said. "One other thing. I didn't get a real good look, but the stone arm Hilda had in there looked like the missing one from the angel statue."

Jessie checked her watch. "I know. Well, let's get to the library like Violet suggested. It's just down the street."

"Can Henry and I wait for you outside?" Benny asked when the children came to the town library.

"Sure," Violet said, setting off with Jessie. "We'll be back in a while."

When the girls found the librarian, they

handed him the piece of paper with the title of the art book they wanted. "My sister and I are interested in this book about a sculptor named Clover Dodge. The book isn't on the shelf. Do you know when it's due back?"

"Clover Dodge?" the librarian asked. "Isn't it funny how some books aren't checked out for ages, then suddenly everybody wants them at the same time? Clover Dodge was a well-known sculptor at the turn of the last century. But her work disappeared, and people forgot about her." The man checked the library computer. "I see one of our local artists, Hilda Stone, checked it out. It's reserved for William Mason next, but I can reserve it for you after he brings it back."

"Hmm, no," Jessie said. "Thank you anyway."

Minutes later, the girls met their brothers outside and told them what they had discovered.

"Wow! So William is interested in Clover Dodge, too," Jessie said. "I wonder if he and Hilda are up to something together with the statues."

"Let's go back to the studio and find out what Hilda has to say," said Jessie.

The rest of the Aldens nodded in agreement. They were always ready for an investigation.

Henry led the way. "While we're walking, Benny can tell you what we discovered while you and Violet were in the library."

Benny couldn't keep his secret another minute. "The scary rock with the door is called Dead Man's Cave, only there aren't any dead people in it," he announced.

Jessie's and Violet's eyebrows shot up.

Henry grinned at the two girls. "Benny and I went to check old maps in the town hall. There are a couple small caves, not very deep ones, on Skeleton Point. One of them is called Dead Man's Cave. The man we met at the general store works in the land records department. He said that a long time ago kids used to hike up there. He'd heard they'd turned the cave into a hideout or a clubhouse. They called it Dead Man's Cave to scare other kids away."

"But we're not scared," Benny said. "We can go there this afternoon, right, Henry?"

"You bet," Henry said. "But first let's see what Hilda is doing with all those skeletons and statue parts from Skeleton Point."

When the children returned to the studio, the STUDIO CLOSED sign was still on the door. This didn't stop the Aldens.

"Hi, Hilda! It's the Aldens," Jessie yelled as she rapped on the window.

Hilda whirled around, startled to see four pairs of eyes staring at her. She opened the door slightly. "What are you doing here? My studio is closed right now."

Violet looked past Hilda. "Oh, so you have the Clover Dodge statue," she said before the young woman could block her view. "Are you fixing it? I'd love to see how."

Hilda stared at Violet. "I'm not here to teach art classes, Violet. I'm here to . . . well, I haven't time to explain."

Henry, who was taller than Hilda, peered right over her shoulder. "Are you fixing the arm from the angel statue, too? Charlotte will be glad you got started on that."

Hilda studied the Aldens' faces. "What do you mean? William was the one who got me working on the angel statue, not Charlotte. He told me she left most of the decisions up to him." Hilda pushed the door to keep the children back. "I really must get back to my work. I'll see you at Skeleton Point later this afternoon."

The Aldens had a lot more to say, but they never got the chance. After she slammed the door, Hilda walked over to the windows and pulled the shades down one by one.

CHAPTER 8

Locked Out!

As soon as the children got on the bike path again, they tried to figure out their conversation with Hilda.

"We didn't get any answers about the Clover Dodge statue," Violet said.

Henry disagreed. "Oh, but we did. Now we know Hilda definitely took things from Skeleton Point and that she doesn't want us to see them. That's got to be the reason she didn't let us in her studio."

"I guess you're right, Henry," Violet said. "I sure wish the statue was back where it belongs. Since it wasn't broken, why did Hilda bring it to her studio?"

The children pedaled along the lake and thought about what to do next.

"Let's have lunch!" Benny suggested. "That helps me figure out things."

"Lunch always solves everything for you, Benny," Jessie said with a laugh. All the same, she slowed down when she came to the sign for the Shady Lake General Store. "You know, if we stop here, we can — "

"Have an ice-cream cone for dessert!" Benny said.

Jessie smiled. "Exactly!"

The children rolled their bikes to a picnic grove close to the dock that belonged to the general store. As soon as the Aldens took out their sandwiches, a flock of ducks decided to join the children for lunch, too. Not a crumb was wasted as the birds waddled under the picnic table. The children hadn't been seated long when another visitor showed up.

"Max!" Jessie said when Greeny's dog raced over to chase the ducks away. "You smelled our ham sandwiches, didn't you? Where's Greeny?"

Benny slid over to pet Max. "Sorry, the ducks ate the rest of my sandwich. Hey, you're as wet as a duck, too. Were you playing in the water?"

"Greeny's boat is docked out there," Henry said, looking at the marina. "He must be at the store getting supplies. Jessie, are you thinking what I'm thinking?"

Jessie nodded. "There's nothing wrong with just going for a walk on the dock, is there? And if we happen to pass Greeny's boat, we might be able to see if he still has that mysterious crate we saw him carry down from Skeleton Point."

The Aldens didn't waste any time. They gathered up their trash and threw it into a nearby basket. Max followed along, hoping to catch a few forgotten crumbs the ducks might have missed.

Benny dug into his backpack for a ball he often carried. He aimed it toward the dock. "Go get it, Max! Let's follow him. Now we have a good excuse to go near the boat."

"Exactly what I was thinking, Detective Alden," Henry told Benny.

As soon as Max found the ball, he trotted out to Greeny's boat.

Jessie had to laugh. "Max is just like Watch. He likes to bring the ball to a special spot then makes us chase him there."

The children ran after Max.

When he got to the dock, Henry stared into the boat. "Greeny sure keeps a lot of stuff in there. Fishing tackle, life jackets, boxes, a couple of toolboxes, fuel cans, and — "

"A skull!" Benny said in a loud whisper. "See? It's in the milk crate, but it's partway covered up."

The children craned their necks, trying to get a better look under the canvas.

Just as a gust of wind began to lift the covering, Greeny appeared. "What are you kids doing?"

Thank goodness for Max. At that moment, he picked up the ball in his mouth and brought it over to Greeny.

"He wants you to take Benny's ball and

throw it," Jessie said. "We were trying to get it back when Max jumped into your boat with it."

Max suddenly dropped the ball, so Benny reached in and picked it up. Max leaped from the boat, and Benny followed him.

By this time, Greeny got in the boat himself. He quickly tucked the canvas cover tightly over the milk carton. "Max, get back here!" Greeny yelled. "Don't throw that ball near the boat, Benny. Got it?"

"Got it," Benny said, walking toward his bike. He felt so upset at being scolded, he forgot all about his ice cream and finishing the game of fetch with Max.

The children quietly pedaled away, not as happily as before. Awhile later, they came to Skeleton Point.

"Let's push our bikes behind those bushes so everything will be safe," Henry suggested. "We can come back for them later."

"What I want to find out," Jessie said as the children began to climb the steps, "is whether William will let us work in Dr. Tibbs's study."

Halfway up, the Aldens searched for the trail they had hiked the day before.

"Hey, where's the secret path?" Benny asked. "Wasn't it right around here?" He skipped a couple steps ahead then came back down. "The skeleton isn't sitting here, either, like yesterday."

"It's almost as if we dreamed up the secret path," Violet said. "Wait! I know why." She pulled away a tangle of prickly holly branches. "These branches covered it up."

Henry still had on his bike gloves. He tossed the thorny branches aside. "Since no one knows we're here yet, let's check Dead Man's Cave before we go to the house."

The Aldens set out on the secret path. Along the way, they looked for the horse skull they had seen the day before. That, too, was gone. They finally located the hideout door.

"Benny, hand me my flashlight," Henry said, peeking into a crack between the door and the rock. "Even if we can't get inside, the door doesn't quite fit over the cave opening. Maybe I can get a look with my flashlight."

Benny rummaged through Henry's bike bag. "Here."

Henry held his flashlight up to the crack. "Gee, it's not much of a hideout," he said. "Our boxcar was way bigger than this. Hey, wait! Jessie, here, take a look."

Jessie took the flashlight. "Wow! That looks like Mister Bones in there. And the horse skull, too. Plus some statues I never saw before. Come here."

Benny could hardly wait. Since he was shorter than the other children, he saw something they had missed. He waved the flashlight over the floor of the hideout. "Look. Footprints."

"They're still muddy," Violet said when she took a look. "Whoever made them was just here."

The children tried hard to pull open the rusty door but had no luck.

"Let's go up to the house," Jessie suggested. "We can at least see if William made those prints. They sure look like his."

"And these!" Henry pointed to a muddy part of the path. "These footprints look pretty new, too. Let's follow them."

When the children returned to the main path, they followed the muddy footprints up the steps.

Henry covered up the secret path with the holly branches again. "I don't want anybody else to find this trail or even know we found it."

When they reached the top, the children saw William heading to the gardening shed with some clippers in his hand.

Jessie caught up to him. "Hi, Mr. Mason," she said. "Oh, your gardening clippers are just like Grandfather's. So are those leather gardening gloves. Were you out pruning brushes?"

William stared at the clippers in his gloved hand as if he didn't know what they were. He ignored Jessie's question. "I thought you kids said you were going swimming today."

"You said that, not us," Henry replied.

"We came here to help Charlotte. Did she call you about working on Dr. Tibbs's skeleton collection? She wants us to count what's in there."

"Waste of time, if you ask me," William said. "Just ship the whole shebang to the medical school and let them do the job."

Violet had something important to tell Mr. Mason. "Charlotte is putting Greeny Owen in charge of the skeletons before she sends them to the medical school."

"Greeny Owen?" William Mason said. "I chased him off here just this morning when I found him wandering around in the house as if he owned it."

Violet had to defend Greeny. "He just wants to protect Dr. Tibbs's skeleton collection. He thinks someone may have taken some of them recently."

William looked at Violet for a long time. "What do you mean, someone took the skeletons? There's such a jumble of bones in there, who would even know if any of them were missing?"

"Greeny would!" Benny blurted out. "And we saw skeletons in the woods, and so did Grandfather and Charlotte."

William laughed. "Well, everybody knows about the Walking Skeleton," he told the Aldens. "Maybe you should tell Charlotte to stay put in her nice little cottage where she won't be scared by skeletons roaming the woods."

"Charlotte isn't scared of skeletons, walking or not," Jessie said. "She's going to fix up Skeleton Point no matter what."

William walked up the broken steps of the reflecting pool. "Well, you can't say she wasn't warned ahead of time."

Jessie checked her watch. "We'd like to go into Dr. Tibbs's study and do what Charlotte asked us to do."

William didn't look too pleased about this, but he nodded anyway. "Suit yourself. If that's what Charlotte wants, feel free."

But the door to Dr. Tibbs's study wasn't open.

Henry pushed the door with his shoulder. "Maybe it's stuck the way it was the other day." When the door didn't budge, he pushed it with his whole body. Still it didn't open. "Know what? There's a lock on it — a new one," he said. "That's why I can't get it open."

Hilda arrived just as the Aldens were heading out to find William.

Jessie went up to her. "Hi, again. Would you happen to have the key to the study? It's locked. Charlotte wants us to get started organizing the skeleton collection."

Hilda looked puzzled. "Locked? Why would anybody lock up those dusty old things? None of the locks inside the house work anyway. Just push the door hard."

"We already did," Henry said. "This lock is new. Did the locksmith finally come? Charlotte sent one out last week, but he got scared off."

Hilda seemed in a hurry and not in any kind of mood to talk with the Aldens. "Well, since you can't get in there, you won't be able to do whatever job Charlotte suggested. Perhaps you should head home until you hear from her again."

The children looked at one another. Why was this woman always trying to make them go away?

Jessie surprised her brothers and sister by agreeing. "Sure. I guess we will go. See you tomorrow."

When the children got outside, Benny was confused. "Why are we going home? Can't we ask her about my photos?"

Jessie put her arm on Benny's shoulder. "We're only going to pretend to leave. We'll sneak to the other side of the house and see what the two of them are up to."

When the children came outside, they waved at William.

"See you tomorrow," Henry called out loudly. Then in a whisper he said, "And probably a whole lot sooner."

Soon the children were hiking through the woods again. As they circled back, they came up with a plan.

"We have to somehow get upstairs without anyone seeing us," Henry said. "That way we'll get a better view around the property. And in old houses, the sound sometimes travels through the heating vents. We might be able to hear what Hilda and William are up to. They seem to spend all their time either outside or downstairs."

The children hid behind some trees not far from the back of the house. A large clearing stood between the house and the woods. Somehow they were going to have to race through the clearing without being seen.

Jessie took the binoculars to check around the property. "Hilda's out talking with William near the reflecting pool. Okay, now. One by one, we have to scoot into the open and go through the back door. Who wants to go first?"

Benny volunteered. "Say when," he whispered to Jessie.

"Now!" Jessie said. "They're facing away from the house. You go, too, Violet. See that room in the tower? We'll meet you up there. If you hear anyone coming, hide behind the furniture. If you get caught, just say you came back to look for Benny's camera." With that, Jessie gave both of the

younger children a little push. They were across the lawn in a flash.

"Uh-oh, duck," Henry told Jessie. "William just turned around. Gee, he's walking this way. I hope he didn't see us."

But William seemed too lost in his own thoughts to notice Jessie and Henry crouching in the bushes. He passed just a couple feet away from them on his way to the gardening shed.

"It's now or never," Jessie whispered to Henry. "Hilda is putting her sketch pad and pencils back into her tote bag. She's going to turn around any minute."

Henry glanced up at the main house. "Look, Benny and Violet are waving us that the coast is clear." Henry grabbed his sister's hand. The two of them raced across the clearing and disappeared into the house.

CHAPTER 9

Skeleton Keys

Henry and Jessie took the stone steps to the tower two at a time. Light on their feet, they didn't make a sound until they reached a landing. There they stopped to catch their breath near a small window.

"We're safe for now," Henry whispered. "William is in the gardening shed. Hilda's outside somewhere."

Jessie leaned against the wall. "My heart is about to burst out of me," she said. "We made it. Let's find Benny and Violet. They were pretty brave getting up here so fast."

Henry and Jessie climbed to the next floor.

"Here's the door." Jessie gave it a push.

She and Henry looked around the silent room. The long, narrow windows didn't let in much light. All they could see were the large white shapes of old furniture covered in sheets. Cobwebs hung down from the tall ceiling.

Jessie brushed one aside so it wouldn't get caught in her hair. "Where are Violet and Benny?"

"Down here," a muffled voice answered from under a lump in the corner.

Henry and Jessie walked over. The sheet moved, then two faces peeked out.

"Hey, you two!" Henry helped his brother and Violet slide out from under a huge bed. "We thought you deserted us."

Benny dusted off his hair. "We thought you were William or Hilda or the Walking Skeleton, so we hid under there."

The children tiptoed to the windows,

which overlooked the property and Shady Lake as well.

"This is perfect," Jessie said. "After William and Hilda leave for the day, we'll go back to get our sleeping bags and backpacks, then tidy up a little."

Henry pulled out his binoculars from under his jacket. "I'm glad I brought these. We can see all the way down to the lake and the driveway from the other side. If anything funny is going on, we'll see it. Uh-oh, Hilda's heading to the house with William."

"Shhh," Violet said when she heard something downstairs. She put her head near the old-fashioned heating vent built into the floor. "Listen. They're in the hallway outside the room below here."

The words weren't too clear, but the Aldens recognized William's and Hilda's voices.

"Now that you have all the measurements, how long do you think the job will take?" the Aldens heard William ask. "I need to get everything done fast."

Hilda didn't answer right away. Her voice

was softer, so the Aldens had a harder time hearing her words. ". . . removing it, getting it to the foundry. Making a copy takes a long time. I wish I never told you about . . . "

The Aldens heard a hand bang against a table. "We don't have a long time," he said, so loudly he almost seemed to be in the same room.

Hilda sounded upset and spoke quietly. The Aldens could catch only a few words. ". . . understand . . . need to . . . back . . . why can't . . . Charlotte . . . now."

"Look, I know what I'm doing," William said plainly. "You don't need to know all the details. Can you do what I asked or not?"

The front door slammed. When the children ran to the window, they saw Hilda run from the house and down the driveway. William left shortly afterward.

"What did she say?" Benny asked Violet.

"I couldn't tell," Violet answered softly. "She mentioned a foundry, so it must have something to do with the statues or something like that. Artists sometimes bring statues to a foundry to have molds made of their statues. After that, it's pretty easy to make copies from the molds."

Jessie opened the window. In the distance she heard one car start, then another. "I think they took the Clover Dodge statue to copy it. But it doesn't belong to them. It belongs to Charlotte. We have to tell her soon."

Henry went from window to window aiming his binoculars down the driveway. "It's probably safe to go out and bring our things up now. That'll give us plenty of time to see what's going on in this house while Hilda and William are gone."

After the children aired the room out, they returned to the beach for their packs and sleeping bags.

That's when Jessie heard a motorboat coming close. "Hide!" she told the other children. "Greeny's boat is headed to the dock. He must be coming from the store. I sure hope Max doesn't sniff us out back here. I have the extra food we brought."

"I've got a good idea," Benny said. "I'll

throw one of our extra sandwiches way over there. If Max finds it, he won't come looking for us."

"Good thinking, buddy." Henry and the other children scrunched themselves behind a thick clump of pine trees and bushes.

Soon they heard Greeny's boat slow down, then stop. The children pushed away a branch ever so slightly. What was Greeny going to do next?

"Okay, Max," Greeny said to his dog. "We're safe for a while. Now's our chance to really clear out a few things — a few crates' worth, at least."

The Aldens barely breathed. They heard Max yipping with excitement when he discovered the sandwich Benny had tossed away from the hideout.

"Maxilla!" Greeny yelled. "Don't eat that! Ugh. Too late. You are nothing but a canine garbage disposal. I just hope you don't get sick. I'm putting you on the leash."

Even on a leash, Max smelled food and came awfully close to where the Aldens were hiding.

"Get up here, Max. I'm not letting you run off again." Greeny led Max toward the steps. "I may not have a whole lot of time."

The Aldens waited behind the pine trees for a very long minute.

"Let's follow Greeny now instead of bringing back our things," Jessie suggested. "He's getting something to put in all those crates I see in the boat. I don't know if it's parts of statues or skeletons or what, but now's our chance to follow him."

The children wondered if Greeny would turn off on the secret path. But he didn't stop at all until he reached the gardening shed. "Sorry, Max, but I can't have you barking and running around. You have to stay in here for now. I'll be back for you later."

"Poor thing," Violet whispered when Max began to whine after Greeny shut the door. "He sounds just like Watch when we won't let him play outside with us."

With Max out of the way, the Aldens felt safer in following Greeny into the house. He unlocked the door to Dr. Tibbs's study.

Shutting the door, he locked it from inside the room.

"I know what we can do," Henry whispered. "Let's go upstairs. If we're lucky, there may be a heating vent up there. Maybe we can see into the room."

By now the Aldens knew where many of the creaky floorboards were and avoided them. They found the room above the study. A thick carpet covered most of it.

"Good, Greeny won't be able to hear us walking around," Jessie whispered. She found a corner where the carpet had been cut to let in the heat through a vent. She signaled the others to come over as quietly as possible and huddle around the vent.

When they looked through the grille of the vent, the children saw the top of Greeny's head directly below. They could see him placing skulls, skeletons, and other kinds of bones into his crates.

The Aldens didn't need to discuss what to do next. In an instant, they ran from the room and down the stairs so fast, Greeny never had a chance to get away.

When Greeny opened the door, the Aldens stood there blocking him.

Greeny couldn't move. In his arms was a milk crate piled with skeleton bones. "I'm not even going to lie about what I'm doing," he told the Aldens.

"Good," Jessie said. "Then maybe you'd better explain what you're doing and why. We already saw one skull in your boat. Where are you going with the rest of them?"

Greeny stared at the children for a long time. "Okay, I might as well tell you the truth. You and your relatives can decide what to do about it. I noticed that after Charlotte hired Mason and that woman — "

Henry had something to say. "Wait a minute. Charlotte didn't hire Mr. Mason; he volunteered."

"Hmmm," Greeny said. "Well, maybe Charlotte should have wondered why an architect would volunteer to do something for free — not that I have any idea. All I care about is Dr. Tibbs's collection. Some of it

has disappeared, and I'd bet anything that those two are to blame."

Henry stepped closer to Greeny. "How do you know that? Right now you're the thief, not Mr. Mason and Hilda. Even Mister Bones was taken. He wasn't yours to take, or anybody's."

Now it was Greeny's turn to look upset. "I know, that's why I'm here. After Mister Bones disappeared along with a wild horse skull from out West, I just knew I had to move the whole collection to a safe place — my cabin. I came in here this morning and installed a lock on the door so nothing else would disappear. There are rare skeletons that Dr. Tibbs collected on his travels around the world. Now I'm taking them for safekeeping. You can tell Charlotte that, too."

"No," Violet said. "If you took these things, you'll need to tell Charlotte yourself — tomorrow when she gets back. We're going to find Mister Bones."

Greeny's mouth opened. "Where?"

"We'll let you know tomorrow," Jessie

answered. "Now please put those crates back and give us the keys. Both of them. We're spending the night here."

Though Greeny Owen was many years older than the Aldens, he obeyed them without any more protest. He carried the crate of skeletons back to the study, pulled the door shut, and locked it. Then he dropped both keys in Jessie's waiting hand and went off to get Max.

The children didn't have Mister Bones just yet, but they had discovered that Greeny Owen was one of their thieves. Now they just had to catch the others.

CHAPTER 10

Alive in Dead Man's Cave

After the sun went down, the Aldens turned on their flashlights. The beams cast shadows everywhere.

"At least we don't have to tiptoe around," Henry said as he and his brother and sisters explored the old house.

The children stayed close together so they wouldn't waste their flashlight batteries. When they came to Dr. Tibbs's study, they hesitated at the door.

"We can go in now that I have the keys," Jessie said to Violet and Benny. "But we don't have to unless you want to."

Henry spotted two camp lanterns on a table in the hall. "Mr. Mason must have left those. Let's turn them on to brighten up this place." Henry pushed the lantern switches. "There, now it looks almost like a people house, not a skeleton house."

Jessie found the keys to Dr. Tibbs's study in her pocket. She unlocked the room.

"Oooh, now I'm not so sure about coming in here," Benny said, taking Jessie's hand. "You go first, Henry."

The children stepped into the room and gazed at the shelves and tables of skeletons. The dim light made the bony shapes seem scarier than ever.

"By the looks of things, about half of the skeletons aren't here anymore," Jessie said. "We know Greeny removed an awful lot of them in those crates."

Violet gazed at the empty window. "I know, but I do think he was telling the truth and that someone else took Mister Bones and some other skeletons. Otherwise, why would he be so upset about them and ex-

cited when we told him we were going to get them back?"

Jessie locked the study again. "Let's look around the rest of the house some more. We'll come back here during the daytime." She took one lantern and led the other children down the hall. When she came to the kitchen, she set the lantern down.

Henry walked over to a wobbly kitchen table where papers and notebooks were scattered on top. "Looks as if Hilda and William set up their work in here." He used his flashlight to get a closer look at the blueprints, notebooks, and papers.

Benny felt braver now that they were in the kitchen and not in the skeleton room. He came over to see what was on the table. That's when he saw something familiar sticking out from one of the sketch pads on the pile. "Look, the pictures I took! How did they get in here?"

Violet had a suggestion. "I don't know, but put them in a safe place right now. When we see Hilda again, tell her you found them."

Benny was glad to have his photos back. "Hey, look at this," he said, turning the pictures over. "Somebody wrote prices on the back. See? The angel statue picture says three thousand dollars. And the picture with the girl statue next to Violet is seven thousand dollars. Is that a lot?"

Henry frowned. "It sure is." He took the picture from Benny and put it down next to Hilda's sketch pad. "The handwriting looks the same."

"Why do you suppose Hilda took Benny's pictures?" Violet asked.

Jessie had a thought. "I have a feeling she or William took them so Charlotte wouldn't have evidence that the statues disappeared while they were in charge."

"Then I'm glad Charlotte and Grandfather are coming here tomorrow morning," Jessie said. "There's a lot to tell them about. Now let's go upstairs and have our extra sandwiches for dinner. We have a big day ahead, and I want to get to sleep early."

* * *

The next morning, sunlight poured into the tower room, waking the Aldens one by one. They yawned and stretched and sat up in bed.

"I feel like a princess in a tower," Violet said. "This bed is so tall and so fancy. I slept just as if I were home in Greenfield."

"Well, I sure didn't," Henry said. "I heard noises while it was still dark this morning, but I figured it was just the wind."

Jessie went over to the window after she heard a car. "Hey, guess who's coming up the driveway. Grandfather and Charlotte." She opened the window and waved. "We're up here."

The children scrambled into their clothes and ran down the driveway.

Charlotte gave everyone a big smile. "Well, you children were very brave to sleep in a house filled with skeletons and no electricity."

Benny shook his head. "It's just half filled with skeletons. Some of them got stolen."

Grandfather looked surprised. "What do you mean? We spoke with William last evening. He didn't mention anything missing. Let's go find him. He's in the house already with Hilda, I imagine. Their cars are parked below."

The children went off to look around.

"No one's here except the rest of Dr. Tibbs's skeletons," Jessie said. "But I think I know where they might be. Follow us."

With the children leading the way, Grandfather and Charlotte followed the shortcut path to the gardens.

Charlotte stared at the empty space where the statue of the girl had been. Her face seemed about to crumble.

Jessie took her hand. "Don't worry. We know where the statue is," Jessie said as she linked her arm in Charlotte's. "We need to cross over the main path, then go into the woods on the other side."

Shortly before the Aldens came to Dead Man's Cave, they heard William and Hilda arguing.

"I don't want any part of this," Hilda said. "You told me you only had copies made so the old statues could be put away safely. You can't sell them or even copies of them. They're not yours."

The Aldens crept along until they reached Dead Man's Cave. The rusted door was open, revealing William, Hilda, and Mister Bones, along with several skeletons and statues the children hadn't seen before.

"Sell what?" Charlotte asked when she stepped forward.

Hilda rushed outside, with William right behind her. He tried to shut the door, but Henry was too quick for him.

"Leave it open," Henry said.

"I'm glad you're here," Hilda said to Charlotte. "I just want you to know that I'm not part of William's scheme."

Charlotte frowned anxiously. "What scheme?"

Hilda spoke clearly. "He was going to make copies of your statues and sell the originals. They were made by a famous sculptor named Clover Dodge, and they're worth a lot of money." Hilda looked embarrassed. "I didn't know what was really going on. I only figured it out this morning

— I followed him here to tell him I was quitting." Hilda pointed toward the cave. "The missing statues are all in there."

Charlotte and the Aldens went in to look around. Sure enough, the Clover Dodge statue sat in a corner, looking sad and out of place. Several statues the Aldens hadn't seen also filled the dark space. Only Mister Bones and the wild horse skull seemed at home in Dead Man's Cave.

"Is all this true?" Charlotte asked William, frowning. "How could you do such a thing?"

William Mason scowled and looked down at the ground. "Yeah, it's all true. I wanted to buy the house myself. It's a gold mine, with all those statues. And some of the rare bones are just as valuable. But you beat me to it — and you didn't even know what you had!"

"If you wanted the house yourself, why did you volunteer to help Charlotte?" asked Henry.

"It's like Hilda said. I figured I could sell the statues and rare bones and make myself some money anyway. I figured you'd never notice if some stuff began to disappear."

"But *we* noticed," said Henry.

William Mason glared at the Aldens. "That's right, you kids started snooping around. I untied your boat to try to keep you away from the house. I even hid some skeletons and bones in the woods, hoping that they'd scare you off — but unfortunately it didn't work."

Jessie looked surprised. "We thought Greeny was the one hiding all the skeletons and bones for us to find."

"I'd never do anything like that," came a voice from behind them. Everyone looked up as Greeny and Max suddenly emerged from behind the trees. Greeny wore black pants and his T-shirt with the skull on the front and the bones on the back. "I followed you here," Greeny said. "I had a hunch these kids knew something about where all the missing bones were. I suspected Mason was behind the whole thing! I'll admit I tried to scare you and your family away from Skeleton Point. I snuck up on these kids the first time I saw them at Skeleton Point and tried to spook them."

"But you can't scare us off that easy," said Benny.

"I figured that out pretty quick," Greeny said. He looked down at the ground. "I'm the one who hid those Halloween skulls in your bike helmets," he said to the Aldens. "And I planted a skeleton by your car, too, Charlotte. I just wanted to save Dr. Tibbs's collection by keeping people away. But I would *never* have used any of the real bones to do something like that — they're too valuable!"

Charlotte moved toward Greeny. They were quite a contrast with each other. Charlotte with her white curly hair, her tweed jacket, and pearl earrings didn't seem to have a thing in common with Greeny Owen in his skull shirt, ponytail, and skull earring. "I'm glad that you told me, Greeny. I hope that now we can be friends — and I hope you know I care about Dr. Tibbs's collection as much as you do."

"Hey, what about Mr. Mason?" Benny asked.

William Mason was slowly backing up, trying to escape from the group without anyone noticing.

When Charlotte turned to look at William Mason, the smile disappeared from her face. "I don't believe we'll be needing your services anymore, Mr. Mason. And you can be sure that I'll be contacting the authorities to inform them of what you tried to do here. I don't think you'll be getting any more architecture jobs anytime soon. Now please leave the property — and be thankful I'm not calling the police."

William Mason opened his mouth to respond, but he couldn't think of anything to say. He spun around and hurried away into the woods.

"Well, children, I guess we'll need to get all these statues and skeletons back to the house," Charlotte said, in a happier voice. "Thank you so much for finding them for me! I had no idea that they were made by a well-known sculptor." She turned to Grandfather. "James, does the name Clover Dodge ring a bell with you?" she asked.

Grandfather looked at his cousin Charlottee as if remembering something long ago. "Dodge? Yes, yes," Grandfather began. "I vaguely recall the name — that was the name of the original family that owned Skeleton Point — before it was Skeleton Point, that is. But I had no idea she was a sculptor as well."

A smile slowly lit up Charlotte's face.

"What's funny?" Benny asked.

Charlotte sighed. "In some ways, I'm better off than I was before all this happened! I have all these valuable statues back, including the ones I didn't even know were missing. And now I have experts — Greeny and Hilda — who can help me bring Skeleton Point back to life."

Benny walked over to Mister Bones. He was hanging just inside the doorway of Dead Man's Cave. "Did you hear that, Mister Bones? You might be coming back to life."

GERTRUDE CHANDLER WARNER discovered when she was teaching that many readers who like an exciting story could find no books that were both easy and fun to read. She decided to try to meet this need, and her first book, *The Boxcar Children*, quickly proved she had succeeded.

Miss Warner drew on her own experiences to write the mystery. As a child she spent hours watching trains go by on the tracks opposite her family home. She often dreamed about what it would be like to set up housekeeping in a caboose or freight car — the situation the Alden children find themselves in.

When Miss Warner received requests for more adventures involving Henry, Jessie, Violet, and Benny Alden, she began additional stories. In each, she chose a special setting and introduced unusual or eccentric characters who liked the unpredictable.

While the mystery element is central to each of Miss Warner's books, she never thought of them as strictly juvenile mysteries. She liked to stress the Aldens' independence and resourcefulness and their solid New England devotion to using up and making do. The Aldens go about most of their adventures with as little adult supervision as possible — something else that delights young readers.

Miss Warner lived in Putnam, Connecticut, until her death in 1979. During her lifetime, she received hundreds of letters from girls and boys telling her how much they liked her books.